"Jake! You've com

Keri couldn't see him—too many people blocked her view—but her instincts took over. Five months ago she could've hidden her news until she'd told him. Now he could see for himself, without any softening of the blow first.

But wasn't he even going to acknowledge her? Keri set her hands protectively on her belly, shielding her baby from the hurt she felt herself. She hadn't realized how much it mattered that he accept her and their—

"What's going on here?" Jake asked his mother.

"We're having a baby shower. Aren't you going to say hello to her?" she asked in little more than a whisper.

Keri managed a smile, knowing everyone expected her to run to him.

The problem was, she could barely manage to breathe, much less run.

"Well, go on, son," Aggie said, grinning. "Kiss the woman you love."

Dear Reader,

At some point in almost every book I've written, a secondary character starts waving his or her hands and shouting, "Talk about me! I've got a story to tell!" I've learned to say yes rather than arguing, because otherwise they make too much noise while I'm trying to tell someone else's story.

THE McCOYS OF CHANCE CITY grew out of this phenomenon. The three McCoy brothers were introduced in the WIVES FOR HIRE miniseries about the Falcon brothers, also of Chance City, a fictional town set in the gold-rush-era Mother Lode region of northern California.

I always love my hero and heroine, but I've also fallen for Chance City, too. It's an ideal place in small-town USA, and yet it has flaws, too, which in many ways make it more perfect. I have a feeling I'm going to be spending a long time getting to know its residents. I hope it's fun for you, too.

Susan

THE PREGNANT BRIDE WORE WHITE

SUSAN CROSBY

Silhouette®
SPECIAL EDITION®
Published by Silhouette Books
America's Publisher of Contemporary Romance

Recycling programs for this product may not exist in your area.

ISBN-13: 978-0-373-65477-2

THE PREGNANT BRIDE WORE WHITE

This edition published by arrangement with Harlequin Books S.A.

Visit Silhouette Books at www.eHarlequin.com

Printed in U.S.A.

Books by Susan Crosby

Silhouette Special Edition

The Bachelor's Stand-In Wife #1912
**The Rancher's Surprise Marriage* #1922
The Single Dad's Virgin Wife #1930
The Millionaire's Christmas Wife #1936
††*The Pregnant Bride Wore White* #1995

Silhouette Desire

†*Christmas Bonus, Strings Attached* #1554
†*Private Indiscretions* #1570
†*Hot Contact* #1590
†*Rules of Attraction* #1647
†*Heart of the Raven* #1653
†*Secrets of Paternity* #1659
The Forbidden Twin #1717
Forced to the Altar #1733
Bound by the Baby #1797

*Wives for Hire
††The McCoys of Chance City
**Back in Business
†Behind Closed Doors

SUSAN CROSBY

believes in the value of setting goals, but also in the magic of making wishes, which often do come true—as long as she works hard enough. Along life's journey she's done a lot of the usual things—married, had children, attended college a little later than the average coed and earned a B.A. in English, then she dove off the deep end into a full-time writing career, a wish come true.

Susan enjoys writing about people who take a chance on love, sometimes against all odds. She loves warm, strong heroes; good-hearted, self-reliant heroines; and will always believe in happily ever after.

More can be learned about her at www.susancrosby.com.

To Barbara Ferris, for your unfailing dedication
to romance novels and authors.
Your enthusiasm is part of what keeps me going.
You truly do make the world a much better place.

Prologue

A bell jangled as Keri Overton pushed open the diner door. Heat hit her first, a welcome break from the biting December cold, then came the distinctive aromas of grilling hamburgers, onions and strong coffee. None of it appealed to a stomach already filled to capacity with butterflies.

She stepped inside and gave the lunchtime crowd a quick inspection, seeking one person, coming up blank. Disappointment but also relief swamped her. After all, what would she say? Her head started echoing with the words she'd practiced. "Hi, Jake, remember me?" Scratch that. There was no way he would forget her. "Hello, Jake. There's something you should know before the rest of the world finds out...." Right. That would go over well.

Keri sighed. She hadn't really expected to find him so easily, but he'd told her about this town, *his* town, and this diner, so she'd hoped—and feared—he would be sitting in a booth, having the burger and fries he'd raved about.

The other patrons gave her curious looks without interrupting their conversations. Chance City was a small tourist town, accustomed to visitors, even the day after Christmas.

Keri took the last stool at the counter, the only one available. From there she had a good view of everyone, not just those seated at the counter, but the ones in the red-leatherette-and-chrome banquettes. She plucked a menu from behind a mini-jukebox, wondering if the townspeople would close ranks if she asked questions about one of their own.

A woman in jeans and black shirt approached, her salt-and-pepper braid disappearing down her back. "Welcome to the Lode. My name's Honey. What can I get you?"

"Do you have ginger ale?"

"We do. Anything else?"

"That'll do for now, thanks."

"All our desserts are homemade daily," Honey said, gesturing toward a glass case displaying pies and cakes like colorful pop art. "Our soup, too. Got chicken noodle today, and clam chowder. Warm you up from the inside out."

Keri smiled at the woman's enthusiasm. "Thank you. I'll keep it in mind." After a minute, Keri stuck the menu in its holder and scanned the room again, more slowly this time. She'd come with a purpose, after all.

He had family here. Would any of them look enough like him that she could identify a relative she might speak to? Could she even remember *his* face well enough?

She tried to envision him. Blue eyes, dark brown hair, tall, fit, sexy. Yes, sexy, even under the circumstances in which they'd met. And lips that had created a firestorm inside her, deep, intense, and thrilling. She'd harbored fantasies about him ever since.

Honey set a glass of ginger ale on the counter as the overhead bell sounded. An elderly woman came in, escorted by two thirtysomething men—one tall, with black hair, the other a little shorter, his brown hair pulled back in a tight ponytail. Many of the customers greeted them. They smiled and said hello in return, but they didn't seem relaxed, especially the man with the black hair, who carried what was no doubt the woman's bright purple cane.

Wait. A man with a ponytail? Keri studied the three people further. They had to be Jake's relatives. The man with the long hair would be his youngest brother, Joe. Which meant the black-haired man was Donovan. They had five sisters, too—a huge family.

Keri set her interest on the older woman. Their grandmother, probably, the woman they called Nana Mae? Keri had heard stories about Jake's whole family for three days. She already felt as if she knew them.

"Oh, look," the woman—Nana Mae—said, her steps small and shuffling. "There's Laura and Dixie. Let's go squeeze in the booth with them."

Dixie? That name didn't just ring in Keri's head, it clanged. Jake had talked about her, too. And her broken engagement to Joe last fall.

Keri looked at the two women in the booth nearest to her as the others slid in, Donovan pulling up a chair to sit at the end. The women were both blonde but different from each other, one being curly haired and earthy, the other sleek and elegant.

"Any word?" the curly-haired blonde asked.

Joe shook his head. A long, uncomfortable silence followed.

"Oh, for heaven's sake," Nana Mae said impatiently. "You can talk about it in front of me. I won't have another stroke. Jake's missing. He's always come home for Christmas, except this year. And he hasn't even called. It's not like him. Something is wrong. We can say that out loud. We need to say it out loud."

Missing? Keri grabbed the counter as her world tilted. Dread scattered the butterflies in her stomach, leaving a ball of ice behind. Her heart pounding deafeningly loud, she focused harder on their conversation, needing to hear what they were saying.

Everyone except Donovan was talking, stumbling over each other's sentences.

"Stop," he finally said, not loud, but forceful enough for the discussion to come to an abrupt halt. "Jake's not missing. He's on an assignment where he can't call us until he's done."

Keri swallowed hard. *Now what?*

"You knew?" the elderly woman asked, her face gone pale. "Why didn't you say something before?"

"I just got word myself. I would've told you after lunch. In private."

Keri slid off the stool and made her way to the table. "Please excuse me, but are you Jake McCoy's brothers, Joe and Donovan?" she asked through the lump in her throat. "And you're his grandmother, Nana Mae?"

"Yes, dear. Who are you?"

"My name is Keri Overton. I…know Jake. I came all the way from Venezuela to see him." She looked at Donovan, deciding he was the one she needed to convince she was telling the truth. "You really don't know how to get in touch with him?"

"No."

Desperately, she said, "Aren't you a big-time journalist or something? Someone with contacts and connections?" Her heart picked up speed again at his icy expression. As if he hated her or something…

Which meant Jake had told his brother about her. About their circumstances. About her being responsible for what had happened to Jake in Venezuela.

"Donny, get the girl a chair," Nana Mae said.

He didn't, but he did stand and offer his.

The room started to swirl a little. She should probably sit and put her head between her knees.

Strong hands grabbed her as she reeled, helping to lower her to the chair. Keri lifted her head to thank him, but he was out of focus.

Nana Mae's voice reached her, however. "You're pregnant."

Keri nodded, which made the room tilt.

"And you're looking for Jake. So I'll take a stab in the dark and say you're carrying Jake's baby."

She needed him, and he wasn't there. Her vision narrowed to one bright point. Sound barely penetrated her deadening world. "Yes," she said finally, right before everything went black.

Chapter One

Five months later

Keri sat in a straight-back chair, eating cake and sipping a tangy fruit punch. The living room of the beautiful old Victorian house was decorated with pink-and-blue crepe paper and balloons. Adding to the vivid atmosphere were lots of brightly dressed women, the same women who had welcomed her with open arms to Jake McCoy's town, even though they only had Keri's word that Jake was the father of her baby, due any day. Fainting was apparently a reasonable measure of truth telling.

Her child wouldn't lack for anything, Keri thought, looking at the colorful array of baby clothes and gear, the largesse of the baby shower now winding down. Some items were new and store bought, others were handmade, repaired or recycled with loving care. Her eyes welled at everyone's generosity.

"Don't you go crying on us again," Dixie Callahan warned from the chair next to her. "I've already had to redo my mascara twice."

"Switch to waterproof," Keri teased the woman, who had quickly become her best friend, the curly-haired blonde from the Take a Lode Off Diner that life-changing day last December. Along with Donovan, Dixie had kept Keri from sliding off the chair when she fainted and had felt proprietary ever since. "It's hormones, Dix. I have no control over them. Anyway, I'm not sad. I'm happy."

As happy as a nine-months-pregnant, thirty-year-old woman could be, she supposed, when the father of her baby hadn't been heard from for five months. Had he been injured during his assignment, whatever that was? Would someone inform them of that—or if he died? Would he ever know he'd fathered a child?

Not that he'd ever sought the role of father. Far from it. Since Keri had landed in town, she'd learned that all three McCoy brothers were commitment-phobic, although the youngest brother, Joe, had been engaged briefly to Dixie last fall after fifteen years of an on-again, off-again relationship that had started when they were high school freshmen.

Keri had moved too often and had lived outside of the U.S. most of her life, so she'd never known that kind of long-lasting relationship. "Having roots" was just a concept to her, not a reality.

"How're you doing, angel?" Aggie McCoy, Jake's mother, asked, bending close, worry in her eyes. Aggie was the world's best hugger, her cushy body like Mother Earth personified, her bottle-black hair and vibrant blue eyes suited to her personality. Keri adored her.

"I'm not in labor, Aggie," she answered with a grin. She'd had two false alarms in the past week, so it was no surprise that everyone was anxious. "How's Nana Mae? Is she tired after all this noise and activity?"

"She's loving every second of your party. Holding court, as you can see. Mama's in her glory. You've been so good for her."

"I'm the lucky one." By the end of Keri's first day in town, she'd been hired as a live-in attendant for Maebelle McCoy, Aggie's eighty-nine-year-old mother-in-law. Nana Mae needed help but would never admit it. Keri needed a place to stay but wouldn't accept charity. Two birds, one stone, Joe and Aggie had pointed out. So, Keri earned her keep by helping out Nana Mae, a job that required more domestic duties than the nursing care that Keri was trained to give.

Aggie took Keri's hand. "I wish with all my heart that Jake would walk through that front door right this second."

"Me, too," Keri said, her heart doing a little dance at the thought. She'd been fretting about his return for what seemed like years instead of months. She just wanted to get the conversation over with, so she would know how he felt and what they would do about it. Even her dreams weren't immune to her tension, having become much more intense lately, more detailed.

"I know, angel. And I know how much you love him." Choked up, Aggie squeezed her hand.

Keri looked at her lap. She couldn't tell Aggie the truth. Jake needed to be the one to decide what he wanted his family to know, not Keri. Still, she felt guilty for keeping things from them. And also worried about him coming home and finding her pregnant. Her emotions were jumbled, changing daily, sometimes hourly.

"Joe's got some empty boxes," Aggie said after a moment. "He'll take everything to Mama's for you. A bunch of us will come along and help you put everything in place. You shouldn't be moving heavy things now."

"Thank you, Aggie. I don't know what I'd do without you and your generous friends and family. You were so kind to host this shower for me."

"It's my grandbaby." She may have eight children and sixteen grandchildren, but this yet-to-be-born child was her Jake's child.

People started saying their goodbyes, the noise escalating, punctuated with laughter. Then Aggie opened the front door as the first few guests were leaving.

"Oh, my word!" She stood utterly still, before suddenly shaking herself, a huge smile spreading over her face. "Jake! You've come home. Jake!"

Keri couldn't see him—too many people blocked her view—but her instincts took over. She stood, looking for a place to hide, panicked, the urge to avoid him stronger than the urge to see him. Five months ago she could've hidden her news until she'd told him. Now he could see for himself, without any softening of the blow first.

And in front of his family and friends.

The sea of people parted, putting her at one end of what felt like a dark tunnel, with Jake at the other end, his arms around his joyous mother, Donovan at his side. Donovan's gaze fired straight at Keri. She ignored it to take in Jake's appearance, her heart sinking. He'd lost weight. His hair hadn't been cut in who knew how long. He looked as if he hadn't slept for…well, months.

Tears pushed at her eyes and burned her throat. *What happened to you?*

He scanned the crowd. Everyone seemed to be holding their breath, waiting for him to spot Keri, but his gaze didn't linger on her, giving her just a brief, blank stare before continuing on.

He wasn't even going to acknowledge her? Or worse, he didn't recognize her? Keri set her hands protectively on her belly, shielding her baby from the hurt she felt herself. She hadn't realized how much it mattered that he accept her and their—

His gaze zoomed back to her and zeroed in, frozen.

"What's going on here?" he asked his mother, who still had an arm around him.

"We're having a baby shower. Aren't you going to say hello to her?" she asked in little more than a whisper.

Keri managed a smile, knowing everyone expected her to run to him.

The problem was, she could barely manage to breathe, much less run.

"Well, go on, son," Aggie said, grinning. "Kiss the woman you love."

Jake's blue eyes lasered Keri's then lowered to her abdomen and back up again.

"Welcome home," she said, her voice shaky, her whole body quivering.

"Yeah, go kiss her, Papa," Dixie shouted. "She's been waiting a long time for you."

Keri could see it was all too much for him. Whatever he'd been doing had only been made worse by coming home to find he was about to become a father. He was thirty-seven, but he looked years older.

He started to speak, then spotted Nana Mae, who had made her way over to him. His eyes went soft. Tenderly, he gathered his grandmother close.

"I missed you," she said, patting his back. "There'll be plenty of time to catch up with the rest of us. You go ahead and greet your girl."

He headed toward Keri. A smile came over his face. He picked up speed.

She trembled with relief. Everything was going to be okay. He was in shock, but he wasn't rejecting her. Okay, good. Okay. Good. Breathe…

Then he was there, within touching distance. He curved his hands around her arms. "Look at you," he said, as if he'd been waiting for her. Then he took her into his arms. She hugged him back—

"I'm going along with this only because of my

grandmother," he whispered in Keri's ear then released her, keeping her hand in his as Aggie started shooing people out.

Stunned, Keri said nothing, couldn't have mustered a word.

"Mom," he said. "You don't need to do that. We'll just step into the kitchen for a minute."

He led Keri away, a journey that seemed to take an hour, during which she plastered a smile on her face. When the door was shut and they were alone, he released her.

"We're in love?" he asked.

"I—"

"And this—" he gestured toward her belly "—is mine?"

"Yes."

"I'm supposed to just believe that?"

"You can do the math. If that doesn't work for you, we can do DNA tests after it's born. I don't need proof, but I figure you do."

"It? You don't know the gender?"

"I decided not to find out. Where have you been, Jake? Why couldn't you call home?"

His mouth hardened. His eyes lost their sheen. "In Venezuela. Nothing like a little kidnapping to stir things up, eh? And revenge. Only sometimes it's not so sweet."

Chapter Two

Jake turned away from Keri's horror-filled eyes. He shoved his fingers through his hair and stared at the floor. All he wanted was some peace and quiet. To sleep in his own bed. To take a shower whenever he felt like it, for as long as he wanted. To eat something he could identify.

Instead he'd been blindsided with a pregnant Keri Overton, the woman who'd consumed his thoughts night and day for far too long. The woman he'd been locked up with—because she thought she knew better than he about how criminals operate.

And then there was his brother. Yeah, Donovan was a dead man. During the almost three-hour drive from the San Francisco airport to Chance City, he hadn't once mentioned Keri, who was not only pregnant but on the brink of giving birth. To *his* child. The result of a one-time, "are we going to get out of here alive?" moment after they'd been kidnapped together, along with her boss/patient. One damned time. And apparently she had everyone in Chance City snowed, convincing them they'd been in love.

"Did you even recognize me?" she asked from behind him.

He blew out a breath. "Not at first." He should have, considering everything, but he'd been caught off guard, especially by her pregnancy. Would never have thought of her in terms of being pregnant. She'd had months to call and tell him that bit of news, all that time from Labor Day until Christmas before he'd gone deep undercover. She hadn't called, so he'd decided he was safe from that worry.

"Would you have recognized *me?*" he countered, facing her.

"I don't know. You've lost weight, and your hair is long. You look older. Maybe it's the beard."

He laughed coldly. Yeah, he'd aged about a hundred years. "Well, you've *gained* a lot of weight, and your hair is much longer, too." She'd had short, straight hair before. Now it was almost shoulder length and wavy. But still a rich, shiny brown, a much deeper shade than her eyes—

The kitchen door swung open, and Donovan came in.

"Thanks for the heads-up," Jake muttered.

Donovan ignored his sarcasm. "Everyone's gone

except family. Everything okay here?" he asked, looking from Jake to Keri.

"You should've called ahead," Keri said. "That kind of shock can send a woman into labor, you know. And what about your mom and grandma? I thought you were in Alaska, anyway."

"I was, until Jake called. We coordinated our flights to arrive in San Francisco at the same time."

"Give us a minute more," Jake said to his brother, not wanting dissension, too tired to participate. He shoved his hands in his pockets, found the small gold medallion he carried with him, rubbed it enough to heat it up.

"Sure," Donovan said. "I just wanted you to know who was still here."

As soon as the door shut, Jake focused on Keri. "Why does everyone think I'm in love with you?"

Her cheeks pinkened. "I didn't think it was necessary to disillusion them. Besides, I was protecting your image."

"And yours."

"Yes. And our child's. Your town…adopted me. But also I needed them, so I let them think what they wanted."

He recalled the excited, hopeful look on his mother's face as she'd waited for him to kiss Keri, the woman he *loved.* He closed his eyes, exhausted.

"You need to sleep," Keri said, touching his arm.

He pulled back. "Where are you living?"

"With your grandmother. I've been helping take care of her."

What now? He couldn't live apart from her. People

would ask too many questions, Nana Mae in particular. He'd spent his life living up to his grandmother's expectations, as had all his siblings. He wasn't about to start disappointing her now.

But at the moment, he couldn't formulate a solid plan. "You need to come home with me, to my cabin. We have to figure out what we're going to do."

"All right," she said, her voice low and raspy.

"We'll make our goodbyes. They won't be happy to have me leave again, but I don't see any other solution." There were details to be worked out, but those could wait.

Yesterday, before his flight home from Caracas, he'd almost gone looking for her but decided against it. If she'd wanted to see him, talk to him, she would've made the effort. She'd told him she wasn't an accumulator—no house, no car, no major possessions. He gathered that meant people, too. So he'd come home, wrung out, needing to hole up for a while. Now he couldn't, at least not alone.

Taking her arm, he moved toward the door, presenting a united front. He was completely aware of her. She was seven inches shorter than him, physically strong, reed slender when she wasn't pregnant, competent as a nurse and caregiver and, beyond question, the most duty-bound person he'd known, which had been the problem in the end.

Touching her now sparked his most enduring memory, however, the one that never left his thoughts—how she was a wildcat in his arms…

His mother's face lit up when they returned. He let

go of Keri to give his mother another hug, then his grandmother, then his sisters. He vaguely recalled seeing some of his nieces at the party, but they were gone now.

"I'm sorry to take your helper away from you, Nana Mae," he said to his grandmother, slipping into the familiar role of grandson, which had never included lying to her before. "Thank you for understanding that I want her with me."

"There was no question about that, Jake. Don't you worry about me. I'll be fine. You go on. We'll give you lovebirds some time."

He spotted his youngest brother then, waiting by the door, and hugged him hard. "You haven't made up with Dixie yet, Joe?"

"Nothing's changed."

Jake couldn't read anything in his voice or expression. "Give me a day, then we'll talk. For now, we're going to swing by Nana Mae's house and pick up some of Keri's things then head to my cabin," Jake said to the happy, still teary-eyed group. "Give us a little time, okay? I'll be in touch."

"My truck's loaded with all the baby gear," Joe said. "I'll drop it off. Dix and a few others are headed to your place now to stock your refrigerator. Then we'll leave you alone."

Jake nodded. "Thank you, all of you, for not asking questions about what I've been doing. I'm sure you're curious, and I'll tell you when I'm up to it." He waited, hiding his impatience, as Keri hugged everyone, then she and Jake went with Donovan to his rented SUV.

He wondered if she would accept that he didn't want to talk to her, either. In his experience, women needed words. He barely had enough for cohesive thought, much less conversation.

And now there was too damn much that needed talking about.

From the backseat, Keri tried to memorize the route to Jake's house as Donovan drove them, but she got lost in the twists and turns of the forested road. She'd never seen Jake's cabin. Aggie had asked several times if she'd like to, but Keri always said no. She didn't think he would like her invading his personal space like that, even pregnant with his child.

Talk about invading personal space.

The thought made her smile, which disappeared when the baby shoved a foot up against her rib cage, making her straighten then arch to accommodate the little soccer player. She grunted a little as she shifted.

"You okay?" Jake asked from the front passenger seat, looking over his shoulder.

"Your child just scored a goal."

He eyed her for a few long seconds. "Did it hurt?"

"It's uncomfortable, not painful."

They pulled into a gravel driveway. Tucked into a grove of trees sat a log cabin, Joe's truck parked beside it. He came out the front door as they came to a stop.

"I stacked all the baby stuff in your office, out of the

way," Joe said. "I'll come back and help put the crib together, or whatever else you need. Just let me know."

"Thanks, Joe," Jake said. He'd held out a hand to Keri to assist her from the SUV but let go of her when she was steady on her feet. "Go on in," he said to her. "I'll be right behind you."

She thanked both of his brothers, then went inside, leaving the door open for him. From the window she watched the three men talk for a minute, then hug, putting a lump in her throat. Would he tell her what he'd been doing all this time? Could he? She thought he'd been working for a private security firm the past seven years, not the government, so how was it he went deep undercover? He'd spent eight years in the army after college, working in intelligence. Or maybe special ops. He was vague about it all. All she knew for sure was he was fluent in a whole bunch of languages, and those skills had been utilized constantly by the military.

As soon as he headed toward the cabin with her suitcases, she turned around and surveyed the room. The ultimate guy space, she thought, all wood and dark colors, a huge rock fireplace, contemporary kitchen, big-screen television. The bedroom and office must be down the hallway. After spending all that time in Nana Mae's house, with its lace curtains and delicate furniture, this was like entering a dungeon. Not a whole lot of sunlight found its way indoors.

There were framed photos spread along the sofa table, pictures of his family, including one that included all thirty-one McCoys, one with Aggie and his late father, a sweet one with his grandmother and a couple in which he wore an army uniform, one with an arm slung over another man's shoulders, the other with a group of ten men. She was glad he left the pictures out in the open, glad he hadn't shut away that part of his life.

Jake came through the open doorway as she waited. She saw a change come over him, in his posture, his expression, his breathing, the reality of being home overwhelming. He set the suitcases down and looked around. His shoulders slumped. After a few long seconds, he moved down the hallway, opened a door and went inside, shutting it behind him, leaving her standing and watching. Silence followed, agonizing silence.

Time dragged. Into the fourth hour she heated a mug of soup and carried it onto the front porch as the sun set. The rich minestrone comforted her in the unfamiliar surroundings, a stark reminder of how little she knew about Jake, even though all they'd done was talk for the three days they were locked in a cell together.

Well, that wasn't all they'd done, given that she'd ended up pregnant—

The screen door opened, and Jake stepped onto the porch. He glanced her way, then stood between the rough-hewn posts at the top of the stairs, arms folded, feet planted, and looked out at his property, with its tall pine and majestic old oak trees, manzanita dotting the landscape, as well, and small boulders. The land was untamed by hoe or lawn mower. There was plenty of greenery, but nothing in bloom, even though it was spring. Keri had come to love the Mother Lode area of Northern California, so different from anywhere else she'd lived.

His shirt was wrinkled, as if he'd not only worn it to bed but hadn't moved an inch the whole time. One side of his face held indentations from the pillowcase.

"It's beautiful here," she said, when she couldn't stand his silence any longer.

He nodded. She waited, wishing for a rocking chair, which would at least give her something to do, but his porch held only two Adirondack chairs.

"There's minestrone soup in the fridge," she said. "I could heat some up for you. If you'd rather have some rotisserie chicken, there's that, and plenty of salad vegetables."

"Thanks. I'll get it when I'm ready."

She started to stand, then realized she couldn't gracefully get out of the deeply slanted chair, so she settled back again. "Your mom told me that you're not here often."

"A few times a year." He stuffed his hands in his jeans pockets and rested one foot on a lower porch rail, still not looking at her.

"So you're usually on the road?" she asked.

He sort of laughed. "On the road," he repeated, shaking his head. "You know what I do for a living."

"I know you do high-level security work. I know you carry a gun. But I don't know why you would go undercover for five months."

When he didn't answer, she said, "Am I not allowed

to ask questions? You intimated I had a hand in it somehow, because of the kidnapping. Don't I have the right to know what that means?"

He finally turned around. Keri rested her hands on her belly, her fingers splayed, protective.

"Let me settle in. I need to get it all clear in my mind first. A lot happened. I do apologize for leaving you alone earlier. Honestly, I didn't have another word in me."

"That's understandable." She shifted her hands, deciding to shift the conversation, too. "The baby's moving."

His gaze dropped.

"Space is tight now," she said, "so it's pretty confined. I can't feel the movements as easily as a month ago. I love lying in the bathtub watching the baby move. It's slow motion, but it always amazes me. Would you like to feel it?"

He hesitated. "Not right now," he said finally.

She didn't push. There was nothing else to say except, "I'm glad you're home."

It was as if someone had turned off a switch inside him. "This isn't home," he said.

"It isn't? You have another house somewhere?"

"No. This is the only house I own, but it's just a house. It's a tax deduction, and privacy when I need to be in town. If it weren't for my family, I would never have bought the place, any place. I travel light."

"I do, too, as a matter of practicality, not choice. You and my parents would get along really well."

There was a long pause. "I imagine I'll find that out for myself sometime in the future."

She pictured him meeting her parents. The *only* thing they had in common with Jake was traveling light. He was serious and controlled. Her parents were…neither. They were good people, though, kind and selfless.

Keri looked around her, patting the chair arms several times, wondering where to take the conversation next. "This feels like a home to me. You have mementos. Pictures. It's furnished and decorated."

"My sister Cher insisted. She always was bossy. Comes from being the firstborn, I think."

Keri was glad to see him finally smile. "I like all your sisters."

"Me, too." He pushed away from the railing. "Minestrone, you said?"

"And chicken. Salad. Sourdough bread." She extended her arms. "Would you give me a hand up, please?"

He hadn't allowed enough space between them, so her belly bumped him. He took a quick step back.

"I know it's a shock," she said hesitantly.

"I should've known something was up, given Donovan's conversation during the drive here. You know he's a journalist, right? I'm used to him asking questions. He always had an insatiable curiosity, that stereotypical "why? why? why?" kid. But he was pushing for more information about the kidnapping today, instead of the job I've been doing that took me out of touch."

"You mean you hadn't told him about us being kidnapped?" She remembered back to the time when she first met Donovan in the diner, and the cold, hard look he'd given her when he found out who she was. She figured Jake had clued him in.

"I did, but I didn't tell him your name."

"He came to his own conclusions, then. I've only seen him once since Christmas. He came home for a wedding. Noah Falcon?"

Jake looked surprised. "Noah got married? That's great. I was here for his brother David's wedding in November."

"Their other brother, Gideon, got married, too. He and his wife are expecting. So are David and his wife."

Jake followed her into the house. "So the Falcon brothers are off the market. That was a long time coming."

"Not as long as for the McCoy brothers," she said, keeping her tone light, glancing behind her.

He shrugged. "I suppose it's a record that'll hold for a while longer. Unless Joe comes to his senses about Dixie."

The fact that he didn't even consider he might get married himself cut into Keri like a knife. She didn't know what she'd expected, but she'd thought it would at least be something he'd think about. As she had.

That's what she got for having expectations. They almost always turned out different from reality.

And if Jake wondered why she hardly said a word to him the rest of the evening, he didn't ask.

Chapter Three

Jake watched Keri keep herself busy all evening. When he wouldn't let her heat up his soup, she disappeared into his office and began going through the stacks of baby items, coming out with tiny clothes and blankets to put in the washer, apparently a requirement before letting a baby's skin come in contact with them. Then she sat at the dining room table to write thank-you notes. They hadn't spoken, unless out of necessity, since he'd come indoors.

He'd probably said something that bothered her, but he didn't know what—and she wasn't talking.

Anyway, he was ready to be alone, and it didn't look like she was headed to bed anytime soon.

He'd channel surfed the television stations as much

as he could stand it, sometimes paying attention for a while, sometimes zoning out, the volume not up loud enough to intrude into his thoughts if he didn't want it to. Sometimes he watched Keri as she made her way to and from the laundry room, her belly a constant reminder of the time they'd shared, and the unknowns of the future.

Donovan would probably insist they get a DNA test, as Keri had offered, to make sure the baby was Jake's, but he didn't doubt her. She may have defied him—with what she considered good reason—but she hadn't ever lied, even when it made her look bad.

"You can have the bedroom," he said when he saw her finally yawn and stretch. It was almost eleven o'clock.

"Of course I won't do that. You need good rest. I'll be fine on the couch." She stacked her thank-you notes neatly, set her pen precisely beside them and came into the living room space.

"You'll take the bedroom," he repeated, an order this time. He needed to be able to move around, not feel hemmed in. To be able to go outdoors if he wanted.

She sat on the coffee table, facing him, their knees almost touching. "Do you need to be alone?"

"Yes."

"All you have to do is tell me, Jake—whatever it is you need. I can't anticipate it. Please just be direct. It'll save us both a lot of grief and confusion."

"All right." Would she do the same?

She headed out of the room but turned around when she reached the hall. "I usually have to get up a couple of times during the night," she said, gesturing toward the only bathroom in the house.

He wasn't sure why she was telling him that. "Do you need a light kept on?"

"No. I just didn't want to startle you."

"I appreciate the warning. I'll keep my boxers on so I don't startle *you*."

She laughed, the pitch almost hurting his ears. He realized he hadn't heard her laugh before. It was a good sound, a healthy one. After months of hearing only men's voices, men who spoke only Spanish, her laugh seemed musical.

She grinned. "Feel free to be comfortable, whatever that means to you."

"And since you've already seen it all…"

"That's not true," she said softly. "It was dark. I only…felt."

A heavy curtain of silence dropped between them, the moment of humor gone because of a memory that could never fade. A child would be born of it.

He'd only felt, too—Keri's long, lean body and firm breasts and smooth rear. Her mouth—God, her mouth.

As if she heard his thoughts, she pressed her fingers to her lips. He stared.

"Good night, Jake," she said, a little breathless, then hurried down the hall.

He didn't expect to sleep. Earlier he'd fallen asleep instantly in his own bed, but it was dark now, and quiet. No sounds of men snoring, or shouting as they slept. No witnessing violence done to others, unable to stop it without blowing his cover. He'd had to keep the bigger picture in mind.

He wished he could snap his fingers and have the memories disappear. Instead they held court in his head. After hours of pacing and prowling, he dropped onto the sofa and turned off the television, stretching out, still fully dressed, and tucking a small pillow under his head. He shoved his fingers through his hair. He needed to get it cut, take away yet another reminder of where he'd been.

He closed his eyes but still saw too much. He probably should take the sleeping pills Donovan had gotten from Doc Saxon for him—except he needed to be able to hear the sounds around him.

He jolted as he heard a door open, then realized it was Keri. Light from the bedroom spilled into the hallway enough that he could see her glance toward the living room as she crossed to the bathroom on a whisper of sound. When she came out, she headed toward him instead of the bedroom. He closed his eyes. The last thing he wanted was to talk.

But after a few seconds he felt something being laid over him—an afghan Nana Mae had crocheted for him one Christmas. He usually kept it on the back of an overstuffed chair.

Jake felt the warmth of the blanket even before she turned away. It smelled…clean.

"Keri." He propped himself up on an elbow.

"Oh, I'm so sorry. Did I wake you?"

"I was awake. Be glad I was."

She frowned. "Why?"

"It's risky, okay?"

"What? To touch you? I didn't touch you."

"The blanket did. Just don't do it. For your own sake."

"All right."

"Have you slept?" he asked.

"Mostly, yes."

"Even though you're in a new place with a man you barely know and are about to give birth?"

"I've had nightmares for months. Tonight I didn't." She gave a little wave and left.

Nightmares. Were hers anything like his? Did she wake up swinging?

Unable to fall asleep, he turned on the television again, settling on a rerun of *Friends*. He must've slept a little, but as soon as the sky lightened, he grabbed his car keys and left the house, needing to get out where he could breathe. Needing not to talk to Keri until he'd given more thought to their situation, wanting to reconcile his memory of her and how he'd clung to it all this time, with the facts before him—that she was here in his hometown. And pregnant.

Primal, protective instincts were overtaking him. He needed to think more logically about everything. Which meant not making small talk first thing this morning.

He drove without a destination, then ended up at Joe's place. Donovan would be bunking with their youngest brother.

Jake pulled up beside the house, one Joe had shared with Dixie for the better part of ten years, on and off. Off again now, though. Jake didn't mind waking Joe up, but he would've thought twice about dropping in so early had Dixie still cohabited.

Joe was already up, however, walking through his garden, a mug of coffee in hand as he deadheaded flowers. His job as a landscaper started early each day.

"Got some more of that?" Jake asked, indicating the mug.

"Donny's here. What do you think?"

Which meant there was always a pot being brewed.

Jake followed his brother into the house, then into the kitchen. "The place looks good. You painted the outside."

"Yeah. Group project."

"Family project."

Joe nodded, a slight, aggrieved smile on his face. He took a mug from the cupboard, poured Jake a cup then they both leaned against the counter and sipped.

"Looks like you're doing most of the gardens in town, Joe. It's all photo worthy."

"I have a crew of twenty now. We're busy all the time. Not just residential but quite a few commercial accounts. It's steady and profitable."

Jake wondered at Joe's low-key responses and tone. He used to be the liveliest brother, the most outgoing and talkative. He looked the same—his shower-wet brown hair was tied back in the ponytail he'd had since he was fourteen, and he wore a T-shirt, shorts and work boots, as usual—but something had changed.

"Think Dixie would cut my hair?" Jake asked.

"I'm sure of it, but are you sure you want her to? She'll ask questions."

"Doesn't mean I have to answer them."

Joe shifted slightly. "Thanks for having Donny tell me what was going on. I worried less. Sort of," he added with a small smile.

"I figure Donny's in risky situations often enough, too. I wanted more than just him to know what was happening. Who to contact. You're the only one who came to mind. I know a lot of extra responsibility has been put on you, Joe, since Dad died."

"I can handle it."

"I know that, too. I just wanted you to know I appreciate it."

"Me, too," Donovan said, coming into the kitchen and heading straight for the coffeepot. "I don't say it often enough."

"True." Turning to Jake, Joe said, "Speaking of extra responsibility and what you've been doing these past months, I don't know how Keri fits in. Where she fits in."

Jake hoped by talking about it, some of the memories would fade. He was tired of living with them all the time. "Keri and I were kidnapped together, along with the man she'd been private nurse to for several months."

"Kidnapped? And this is the first I'm hearing about it?"

"I'm telling you now, Joe. Hidalgo Escobar, Keri's patient, had been on the waiting list for a liver transplant for months."

"In Venezuela?"

"Yes. I was on an assignment there and had come across intelligence that Escobar was a target of a hard-core kidnapping group, one that makes a living off ransoming people. I tracked down Escobar and warned him—and Keri, too, since she was always with him. They were supposed to wait for a helicopter to take them to the hospital when they got the call that a liver had been found for him. The helicopter never showed, so they headed to the hospital, a two-hour drive from Caracas."

He and Keri had argued that first time he'd met her, but that wasn't something he would tell Joe. In the end, she hadn't taken his advice, had specifically gone against it, in fact, because she felt she had to, that Escobar's survival depended on it.

"She didn't call you?" Joe asked.

"They hadn't hired me, but when the copter didn't show, she *did* call me." He'd told her to stay put, but she'd insisted the transplant team wouldn't wait long before contacting the next person on the list. "What was I supposed to do? Let her take Escobar alone? Unfortunately, for medical reasons, she refused to wait. I met them on the road to Caracas, but it was too late. We were accosted by armed men, forced into their van, blindfolded and taken to a location miles away."

Jake dumped his coffee down the drain, the taste suddenly bitter. "It was an inside job, involving someone at the hospital who knew all the details—Escobar's address and when he would be on his way. The helicopter was prevented from taking off. My presence was a surprise, but everything else was according to plan. They knew they could get a lot of money for Escobar anytime, but especially right at that moment, when his life depended on it."

Joe joined him at the sink. "So he was ransomed?"

"Within hours."

"But not you?"

"Or Keri." The leader of the gang, a loose cannon named Marco, had taken a fancy to her. They'd decided to demand a ransom for Jake but keep Keri for a while. Jake wouldn't give them a contact for himself. He wouldn't leave Keri alone, period.

"What happened?"

"One of the kidnappers got us out." There was much more to it, of course, an internal power struggle, a disgust of Marco's intentions by José, the man who helped Jake and Keri escape. José had been killed for it.

"So, when you were home over Labor Day last year," Joe said, "this had already happened? That was why you were keeping to yourself so much?"

"Yeah."

"How does Keri fit in? Why didn't she come back with you?"

Jake rested a hand on Joe's shoulder. "That's all I want to say about it for now. And it's between us, okay?"

"Hey. Goes without saying, Jake."

The sound of the front door stopped further conversation.

"Where are my boys?" Aggie's voice filled the house.

"In the kitchen, Mom," Joe called out, then fired a "good luck" look at Jake.

Aggie breezed through the doorway. She was a vibrant sixty-seven-year-old widow of ten years with a great laugh and a big heart. The McCoy children had been raised to know unconditional love—and little privacy, which some of her children handled better than others.

"I saw your car out front," she said to her oldest son, passing him a plastic container. "Apple turnovers."

"I was coming to see you next," Jake said honestly, giving her a hug.

"Isn't this a rare treat, having all my boys here at the same time." She accepted the mug of coffee Donovan handed her. "I expect you'll be gone soon, though, hm, Donny?"

He shrugged. "I'm thinking I'll hang around a while longer, if Joe doesn't mind. Or maybe I'm cramping your style?"

Joe looked over the rim of his mug at Donovan. "Nana Mae's going to need some help now that Keri has moved out."

Jake laughed. He'd missed this, being with his family, the comfort of familiarity, even as he didn't know them as well as he used to or should.

"Didn't you hear?" Aggie said. "Dixie's moved in with Mama to help."

All eyes turned to Joe. Jake wondered why his youngest brother and the love of his life, Dixie, hadn't managed to find their way back to each other this time.

They'd never stayed apart more than a month before, and this made six months.

"Good of her." Joe turned away as he spoke. He rinsed out his mug and set it in the sink, the motion deliberate. "Well, some of us have to work." He kissed his mother's cheek and grabbed a turnover from the container Jake opened and held out to him. "See you all later."

Donovan excused himself, as well, after also snagging a turnover. Jake set the container on the counter. He didn't think his stomach was ready for the high-fat, high-sugar treat. "Do you want to go into the living room?" he asked his mother.

"Sure. Bring those things along. You need to eat, Mr. Skin and Bones."

He guided her out of the kitchen. "Not now, Mom. I appreciate your making my favorite, though. I'll take them home with me." They sat on the sofa. He saw the unspoken maternal concern in her eyes. "You look like you've dropped a few pounds, too."

"Not too much room for food in a stomach when it's full of worry."

He took her hand. "I'm sorry. I wish I could've gotten word to you."

"Where were you, son?"

He debated how much to say. "Helping take down a kidnapping ring."

Her face paled but her gaze held steady. She wasn't one to crumble. "One you infiltrated, I suppose. I've seen enough movies and TV shows about that kind of thing."

"Then you have an idea." Although she really couldn't. No one could imagine what went on unless they lived through it.

"And that you probably can't say more than that," she added authoritatively.

"You got it."

"We kept your Christmas presents," she said, her eyes lighting up. "I figure we can have a Christmas-in-May party."

He smiled at that. "Give me time to shop first."

She squeezed his hand. "Your being home is gift enough. And the new grandbaby you're giving me." She settled herself in the sofa cushions. "How'd it feel seeing Keri? I'll bet you were surprised at how big she is."

The understatement of the year. "Yes."

"We think the world of her, you know."

"She told me you all adopted her. I appreciate everything you did."

"She's a sweetheart. And so brave."

Those particular traits of hers, along with extreme stubbornness, were what had led to their capture. "You'll get no argument from me."

"So when's the wedding?" Aggie asked, lifting her mug.

Wedding? "Uh, we haven't talked about it yet."

"Don't you think you need to get to it? She could pop any second. She's already had two false labors."

"She has?" He didn't know exactly what that entailed.

"A real trouper, that one." Her eyes, deep blue and direct, took aim at his. "We've had a few 'early' babies in our family, but none as close to the wire as this one."

And no divorces. Jake didn't say the words out loud, but they clanged in his head like the bell at Notre Dame, reverberating, deafening. "When Keri and I decide what we're going to do, you'll be the first to know."

Aggie pursed her lips. "I don't see how there could be any hesitation—or doubt."

"Just give me a chance to breathe, okay?" His jaw hurt, his hands clenched.

After a long silence, Aggie said, "How is Keri feeling this morning?"

"I don't know. I left before she woke up." He could see her debating what to say. He was, after all, one of her children who ignored what she called her "mother's right to know," as all eight siblings had been told forever. To forestall any unwanted advice or recrimination, he stood. "I'll go home right now and check."

"Would you like to come to dinner?"

He forced himself to keep his voice level, reminding himself that she didn't understand all he'd been through and that he needed time and space—something Keri had recognized. Score one for her. "Not tonight, okay, Mom? I'll talk to you later."

Jake scooped up the container of turnovers, then went out to his car. He headed up the winding road, again with no particular destination in mind, only a need for his previously unappreciated freedom, and solitude of his own choosing.

And yet ten minutes later he found himself pulling into his own driveway.

He had responsibilities he couldn't ignore now, no matter what else was on his mind.

He could almost see his mother's approving nod and feel his late father's pat on the back, the weight of his responsibilities made even heavier by parental expectations—and those of his grandmother, who hadn't yet had her say.

Chapter Four

He hadn't even left a note.

Keri kicked a pebble and watched it tumble down the slope behind Jake's cabin. He'd taken off this morning without extending even the most basic courtesy of telling her he was leaving, and also stranding her without a car.

She toed another pebble loose then kicked it, not giving it her all. The baby had dropped recently, shifting her center of balance, and there was nothing to grab hold of to stop her from falling.

She grumbled at the ground, feeling handcuffed by her isolation after months of living in the easy company of Nana Mae, and with Aggie right up the block, not to mention Dixie only three streets away.

Keri had constantly thought about seeing Jake again, her fantasies about their reunion mushrooming out of proportion with time and distance, and pregnancy, of course. Doesn't every woman want her baby's father in her life? And it wasn't just her, but his family and friends' steady assurance that everything would be perfect once Jake came home. She'd begun to believe it herself, needing something to hold on to.

The reality hadn't matched the fantasy, which made the letdown even harder.

Keri heard a car approaching. Through a smattering of trees, she spotted a black SUV as it made its way toward the house. She rounded the corner of the house as Jake got out of the vehicle. She had a whole lot to say to him, then stopped short when she saw him—his too-lean body and too-tired face stark reminders that he'd been through some kind of hell.

She didn't want to fight with him or add to his burdens.

"Good morning," she said, as they walked toward each other.

His shoulders relaxed a little. "Morning. You okay?"

"Yes, I'm fine, thanks. How about you?" They sounded like strangers. Well, technically they were. Strangers who'd slept together once, no matter what ensuing hopes had come of that for her.

He passed her a plastic container. "Apple turnovers. Mom made them."

"Yum." So, he'd gone to visit his mom. Keri forgave him for leaving without a note. "Did you have breakfast with her?"

"I wasn't hungry." He gestured toward his side yard with his head. "You were out for a walk?"

Nothing else to do. She stopped the words from escaping. "I walk a few times a day."

"Did I interrupt it?"

"No, I'd been out for a half hour. I'm ready to sit for a little while."

They turned toward the house at the same time.

"You've been healthy, then?" he asked, matching his stride to hers.

"Exceptionally. I adore your Doc Saxon."

His brows raised. "He delivered me. He must be ninety by now."

She laughed. "Seventy-two, I think. He's looking for a replacement, but it's hard to get anyone to come to a community this small. I told him after the baby was born, I'd help him search, maybe even work a couple days a week."

Jake turned a sharp gaze on her. "I'll provide for you and the baby."

Her heart slammed into her sternum. What did that mean? Provide in what way? "I don't want to lose my nursing skills," she said as they went into the house. "It's not about the money."

"Isn't it? You don't own anything."

"By choice." She took off her sweatshirt and hung it on a hook by the front door, then went into the kitchen to make some tea. "I couldn't accumulate anything, since I moved from job to job so often. If I wanted those things, I could have them," she added, waiting to see if by "provide" he meant he would offer her money to set her up somewhere and guarantee he'd get to see the baby. As if she'd keep the baby from its father. Or maybe he'd meant he intended to be part of their future, although she'd always assumed that would happen. He was a good man, not one to shirk his responsibilities.

"I've hardly ever had to spend any money, Jake. I've got a ton. Well, that's an exaggeration, I guess, but I could buy what I need."

"Yet you stayed with my grandmother."

"Again, a choice I made. We needed each other. Money wasn't the issue." She lit the burner under the teakettle. "Can I fix anything for you? Coffee? Breakfast?"

"Have you eaten?"

She'd had a bowl of cereal, which was enough, but she decided he wouldn't let her fix him anything if she wasn't eating, too. He needed to eat. "I thought I'd have some scrambled eggs and toast. Would you like some?"

"Yeah, thanks. If you'll do the eggs, I'll do the toast."

"That's a deal." As she washed her hands, she felt him come close. He stopped maybe a foot behind her, but her sense of him was so strong, her pulse leaped. If only she could turn to him, be held for a while. He'd held her in that dark, dank, frightening place all those months ago, when she'd panicked in a big way, thinking they would never get out alive. He'd taken her in his arms and held her tight, soothing her even though he'd been furious at her, too, for getting them into the situation to begin with.

Eventually he'd kissed her as she crumbled in fear, his mouth warm and comforting at first, then hot and needy, stopping her tears, giving her different reasons to shake and quiver.

And after the wild and intense sex, he'd held her as she slept well for the first time since they'd been kidnapped....

"What's wrong?" he said from behind her, passing her a hand towel.

Her belly brushed his as she turned and leaned against the counter. She dried her hands, meeting his curious gaze, careful not to look at his mouth, his sexy, comforting mouth. "I zone out sometimes. Don't mind me. It's hormones."

He didn't move out of her way. "Mom said you had false labor?"

"I didn't go to the hospital or anything, but I've had some moments." She patted her belly. "I think this one's been waiting for you to get here, so that you could take part in the birth."

His jaw went slack. She probably shouldn't have assumed he would want to be in the delivery room.

"Do you faint at the sight of blood?" she teased, needing to lighten the tension.

"Hardly." He nudged her aside to wash his hands, keeping his back to her.

She came so close to setting her hands on his back and massaging away his tension. Would she feel his ribs, now that he'd lost so much weight?

She passed him the towel then went to the refrigerator for eggs.

"I'll be there, Keri. When the baby is born."

She squeezed her eyes shut for a second, relieved. "Okay." She cracked eggs into a bowl. "At some point today, would you take me to Nana Mae's so that I can pick up the rest of my things and her car?"

"Her car? Why?"

"She's been letting me use it until I find what I want to buy."

"I have a car," he said in a tone implying it was obvious.

It was the perfect opportunity to get after him for leaving her without transportation earlier, but she didn't. "Which means I'm at the mercy of your schedule. Nana Mae's car will do fine."

"Last I knew, she still had that old Geo."

"She still does."

"Even though she hasn't driven in fifteen years."

"Even though. She's sort of a personal rental-car business. Your nieces and nephews have needed it now and then, so she's loaned it out." Keri heard the crinkle of bread wrapper as he prepared to fix the toast, making everything seem so homey, when it was far from that. They were polite with each other, treading carefully. "It's a cute little car, and it runs great."

"No."

"No, what?"

"You're not driving it. It's too small. Too light."

"I've been driving it since I got here, Jake."

"Joe should've let you use my car."

"He offered it."

"Ah."

She turned toward him. "Ah?"

"Stubborn."

"You say that like it's a bad thing."

He met her gaze. They challenged each other with their eyes. "Are you even supposed to be driving at this point?" he asked.

"As long as I can be ten inches away from the air bag."

He studied her, his gaze traveling down her body and back up. He didn't need to say anything to get his point across.

Silence crackled between them. She finished cooking the eggs. He set toast on the plates, then carried them to the dining table.

After eating a few bites, she said, "Do you seriously think I would put my child in danger?"

"Humor me."

Should she? Dixie had told her recently that damsels in distress were Jake's specialty, so his overprotectiveness was apparently his default mode. She should probably expect him to come from that position on every issue. Certainly it had been the case in Venezuela, before, during and after the kidnapping.

"I measure the distance every week, and today would be the day to recheck," she said, trying but not totally succeeding in keeping her tone from being snippy.

He looked ready to laugh. She waited, her arms crossed. Then, just when he seemed about to say something, the doorbell rang.

He shoved away from the table and went into the living room. Keri picked up the empty plates. She couldn't see who was on the other side of the door, but she could hear a woman say, "I didn't even get to hug you yesterday."

"I guess Joe called you," Jake said, opening the door wider, letting Dixie in, giving her a quick hug.

Dixie waved at Keri, then held up a small tote bag. "I brought everything I need, but you'll need to wet your hair."

"Sure. I appreciate this, Dix."

Dixie watched him walk away, then moseyed into the kitchen, her curls bouncing. She was a couple of inches shorter than Keri, and curvier, if one didn't count the pregnancy. "So. How's it going?"

Keri slid plates into the dishwasher. "It's fine."

"Fine," Dixie repeated in the same neutral tone, frowning. "That's a mild word, especially since the tension was as thick as thunderclouds when I walked in the door."

"Just a normal period of adjustment." She shut the dishwasher and looked for something else to do. Dixie was her best friend, but Keri had confided little about how she'd met Jake, even though she'd ached to tell someone. She wanted to talk about how she felt, get someone else's feedback to help her see her situation with more clarity. Help her sort through the push-pull of her emotions.

"Is he okay?" Dixie asked.

"I can't tell you. It's up to him."

"Then we'll never know. He and Donovan are as closemouthed as they come."

"Which is one reason why they're both good at their jobs. Would you like some tea?" Keri asked sweetly, making Dixie laugh.

"No, thanks. I think I'll take a chair out to the porch. No cleanup, that way."

"Good. He needs sunshine."

Dixie took Keri's hand. "He went through some kind of hell, didn't he?" Dixie asked quietly.

After a moment, Keri nodded, not knowing the details, but it only took looking at him to see that much.

Jake rounded the corner, his long hair dripping wet, a towel over his shoulders. "You remember how I used to have it cut?" he asked Dixie, ignoring Keri.

"Of course."

He grabbed a chair and carried it outside, leaving Keri and Dixie to wonder if he'd overheard their conversation, and if so, how much of it. After a few seconds, Dixie shrugged and followed him.

Keri wiped down the countertops, checked to see what she could make for dinner later and then was at a loss. The kitchen was clean. She'd finished her thank-you notes. She didn't feel like watching television, so she wandered out the door. Jake's eyes were closed, the sun on his face, as Dixie snipped away, the usually direct and forthright woman as quiet as Jake.

Keri didn't think she made any noise, but he opened his eyes. She couldn't read his expression. All she knew for sure was he was exhausted. How much had he slept last night? She'd heard him prowling several times, heard him open the front door and, she assumed, go outdoors a couple of times.

"So, you moved in with Nana Mae," Jake said to Dixie.

"Really?" Keri said before Dixie answered. "Oh, I'm so relieved. She's tough, but she really shouldn't be alone all the time."

"That's how I felt. It also means I can quit working for my parents at the hardware store, and fast-track cosmetology school. They're letting me switch from the part-time program to full-time. I'll be done four months from now instead of eight."

"You haven't graduated?" Jake asked, as if horrified. He ran his fingers through his hair. "Still there. Okay."

Dixie gave him a little shove. "I've been cutting hair since I was fourteen."

"Isn't that about the time you and Joe met? Hm. I'm thinking there's a reason he wears his hair long."

Keri smiled, happy to see him teasing Dixie.

Dixie seemed satisfied with the haircut, then studied his face. "I can shave that beard, too, if you want. Or at least trim it close enough for you to shave comfortably."

"A trim would be good."

After a few minutes of careful snipping, she pulled the towel from his shoulders and shook it. "Some lucky birds will be feathering their nests today with long brown hair."

The haircut should have made him look like the Jake that Keri remembered, but with the beard down to just a stubble, she could see even more starkly how drawn his face was. She whispered, "Excuse me," and went inside the house and into the bedroom. She sank onto the bed.

After a couple of minutes, Jake joined her, sitting on the bed, but not too close.

"Hormones again?" he asked.

She could've grabbed at that as an excuse, but she didn't. "I need to know what happened to you."

Chapter Five

Jake also had a need to open things up between them. He'd been home less than twenty-four hours, but it felt like days, like they should've already talked everything through, when actually there'd been little time to do so.

No more excuses. "Let's go into the living room." He needed to be in a bigger space, somewhere with views of the outdoors.

He followed behind her. She was wearing those pants that come to just below the knees, and a formfitting, bright yellow top that made a sunny silhouette of her belly. Her shiny brown hair brushed her shoulders. He clenched his fists against running his hands down the soft length, and dipped his hands into his pockets instead, feeling for the medallion that had become his talisman.

He wanted to hold her. Ached to hold her. He hadn't known how important physical contact was until he'd been denied it. He'd never been much of a toucher, a complaint he'd heard through the years, wasn't one to hold hands or "cuddle" after sex, another oft-recited criticism. He didn't have time for it. He always had work to do or a need to decompress after a hard case. Sex was important, and often part of the decompression, but relationships weren't.

And now here he was, about to become a father, one of the most important relationships a man could have, one that would last a lifetime.

Jake watched Keri sit in a rocking chair that someone had provided and which looked out of place with the rest of his furnishings. Someone wise, he decided, when she leaned back, ran her hands down the arms and closed her eyes for a moment, as if that was all she needed to settle—or prepare—herself.

"Okay," she said.

"I've spent the past five months helping to shut down one of the biggest kidnapping rings in South and Central America."

Her eyes widened. "I thought you were with a private company."

"I took a leave of absence." In fact, he hadn't drawn any salary for it. "I hooked up with the governments of several countries. We formed teams, infiltrated branches of a far-reaching kidnapping business that took in millions weekly. Obviously I couldn't go anywhere near the group that had taken us, so I went to Nicaragua."

"Why? Why would you do such a thing?"

He sat across from her, rested his arms on his thighs and leaned forward. "A man died for us, Keri. I needed to avenge his death or I never could've lived with myself."

"Who died? Oh, no! Not José? The man who helped us escape?"

"Yes."

She covered her mouth with both hands. Jake made the decision then not to tell her José had been protecting her, not him. Or about how the leader, Marco, had planned to make her his—for as long as he would've been interested. Given that she never would've been cooperative, his interest wouldn't have lasted long.

She didn't need to know that—not now, not ever.

"Five months doesn't seem like enough time to accomplish something that big. To infiltrate and establish trust," she said.

"You're right. I joined an ongoing task force. They were already ramping up the investigation because the press was finally starting to make note of the kidnappings, something that had been almost accepted in the past. The kidnappings had become more violent."

"Did you shut them all down?"

"That would be impossible, and more will start up, probably already have. But we brought in hundreds of men in six countries. A lot will never see the inside of a jail, but many will, mostly the chiefs."

"Marco?"

"Yeah."

"Which doesn't change the fact that José is dead.

And it's my fault, isn't it, because I wouldn't wait for you to come get Señor Escobar." She shoved herself out of the chair.

It was time to stop the blame, he decided, watching her pace from the fireplace to the front window and back. He shouldn't blame her for going above and beyond the call of duty, something he'd done himself many times, for what he'd also thought were the right reasons. How could he fault her? Yes, he'd been kidnapped, too, because of it. But she'd also escaped further harm because he was there. His presence had been necessary.

He would stop blaming her. And she needed to stop blaming herself.

"We need to let go of it all," he said, joining her. "We both need to move on."

Her eyes searched his. He saw deep compassion and caring, something he'd seen from the first time they'd met, but mixed now with guilt.

"I need to know if you were mistreated," she said.

"I was a low man and therefore given the worst jobs to do. Everyone was knocked around some. It's a way of life. But aside from eating really bad food and sleeping on the floor, I wasn't mistreated, no." There was more, so much more, but why put those thoughts in her head? It was enough that they were in his.

"I'm so sorry," she said, like a quiet scrape across sandpaper. "Can you really move on? Leave it behind?"

"That part of it, yes. But I need to know why you didn't contact me and tell me about the baby."

"You mean before you went undercover?"

"You had four months, Keri."

"I didn't realize I was pregnant. I know that must sound impossible, but the trauma of the kidnapping had a physical and emotional impact on me. I stayed with Señor Escobar during his recovery, but I was healing, too. I left as soon as I could manage. I had to find someone to replace me first. Then I came here. I was sitting in the Lode when your brothers and Nana Mae walked in. Everything happened so fast after that. After a trip to see Doc Saxon, I was moved into Nana Mae's house and had been there ever since."

"What did you tell everyone about us?"

"Not much. They took what little I said and turned it into some kind of fairy tale. Because your mother and grandmother needed to hold on to a piece of you, I let them all believe more than was really there."

"And you? Did you need to hold on, too?"

"I held hope," she said after a few beats. "I already had a piece of you growing inside me."

"You could've kept it all to yourself. Lots of women do."

She frowned. "That would be wrong. You deserved to know you were going to have a child. I couldn't have justified not telling you, not for any reason."

Duty bound, he thought. Always duty bound. They made quite a pair.

"What do your parents say about the pregnancy? I assume you've told them by now."

She actually smiled, although a little grimly. "I was

born six months after they married. What could they say?"

"Where are they now?"

"In Peru. They're taking a new assignment in a month, probably in Lesotho, Africa, helping with the AIDS crisis there. They called this morning. They're going to come visit on their way and meet their grandchild."

He scratched his head, was startled by the short length of his hair. "Then I guess your father won't point a shotgun at me."

"I wouldn't be too sure about that. They might both be throwbacks from the hippie era, but they did marry, Jake."

"Meaning?"

"I don't know how they're going to feel about it all, now that you're home and available, so to speak. I'm their little girl, no matter how old I am."

Great. So a month from now he would face her parents, who'd spent their adult lives doing good all over the world—and would probably expect him to do good, too, as in marry their daughter. And they might not approve of their grandchild's father traveling into hot spots all over the world, a world that was changing, the risks intensifying.

"Are you all right?" Keri asked.

Sure. He didn't say the sarcastic word aloud. "If you want to get the rest of your things from Nana Mae's house, let's go now. I'll get a tape measure, too, and we can see if you can fit behind the wheel."

Her chin went up a notch. "I have an appointment with Doc Saxon at one o'clock. Would you like to be there?"

No. "Yes."

"I also have some pictures from the ultrasound I had a few months ago. Do you want to see them?"

"Maybe later." His sisters had shoved plenty of ultrasound photos in his face, given the fact they had sixteen children between the five of them. He didn't figure these pictures would be any different. He crossed his arms. "They expect us to get married, you know," he said.

"They, who?"

"My family. Everyone in town."

She was quiet a couple of seconds too long. "Which is a normal expectation, since they all think we're in love and there's a baby involved."

"Do *you* expect it?"

Again she hesitated a few seconds. "The only expectation I have at this time is to deliver a healthy baby. The rest will work itself out."

Did she know that no one in his entire family had ever divorced? Had she not heard that? She must have. It was legend in Chance City. Everyone called his brothers and him "the men who wouldn't commit"—especially Joe, because he'd courted Dixie for so many years without committing. It was more than that, and mostly tied to Nana Mae, the moral compass of the family, and her expectation that once you married, that was it. You married for life.

"Jake?" Keri said, leaning closer to him. "You need to remember that they don't realize we hardly know each other. We went through a horrible experience and we found solace in the midst of it, but it was all in…" She seemed to search for the right words.

"The heat of battle?" he offered.

"Yes. Emotions were heightened. The will to survive colored everything. It wasn't real."

He gestured toward her belly. "That says otherwise."

Her mouth tightened. "Yes. But it's only one factor."

"Are you saying you don't want to get married?"

"I'm saying if we do, it'll be because it's what we both want. And if we take that pressure off ourselves, it would let me relax around you a lot more. I'd like to have fun with you. Laugh a little." She set a hand on his chest, enjoying how his muscles contracted at the slight touch. "I know you have some healing to do. You need to eat and rest and exercise. You also need to relax. So, don't worry about me. About what will happen. Not now. There's time."

Her words, and the gentle tone in which she said them—her nurse voice?—went a long way toward relieving his tension, not like a balloon with a slow leak, but one that hit a power line and popped, letting out all the air at once, almost knocking him to the ground.

She was too understanding, too kind….

Cynic. The word bounced in his head. He'd seen the worst in people, and sometimes the best. This was a honeymoon phase with Keri at the moment, like all new relationships. Theirs had just started at a different point from most.

He found the medallion again, which settled him. "If you're ready, we can head into town and do whatever needs doing before the doctor's appointment. I'll grab that tape measure."

She laughed, sounding a little nervous, but he noticed she didn't try to stop him, didn't say okay, that she'd let him do all the driving.

They would see who won this round.

They found Nana Mae on her sun porch eating lunch, a grilled cheese sandwich and a cup of tea, no sugar, which she always drank hot, never iced, no matter the season. As Keri made small talk with her, Jake noticed his grandmother was using a mug and holding it with hands that shook a little. One of his most vivid memories of her, aside from playing a million games of Yahtzee, was of her pouring tea from a flower-painted pot into matching teacups, the set a treasured wedding gift.

He recalled being made to attend her tea parties with some of his sisters. Nana Mae always poured, sat back, held the cup close to her face, shut her eyes and let the aroma soothe her before she took a sip.

Ritual.

When he was ten or so he'd refused to attend the event anymore. He knew it had hurt her feelings, but he didn't want his friends knowing he drank out of those girly cups. He hadn't even visited her much after that, just saw her at family events or occasionally delivered something from his mom or dad. Now he regretted that.

Did he have any rituals himself? He didn't think so. His life changed almost daily. He moved from place to place, sometimes danger to danger, quietly doing jobs most people never knew existed, mostly on foreign soil. After graduating from college, he'd spent eight years in Army Intelligence, was fluent in seven languages, had also learned to fly most kinds of small planes and helicopters. His firm's name and number were in the databases of government leaders, corporations and even some celebrities from around the globe.

He thrived on the adrenaline rush that came with each experience and his ability to control it.

Who would've thought a kid from Chance City, California, would end up—

"That wall won't tumble if you move away from it, Jake," his grandmother said, her eyes twinkling. She patted the chair beside her. "Come sit while Keri packs up."

Dutiful, he sat. "I was just remembering your tea parties."

Her face lit up. "Were you? I'm glad."

He covered her hands, wrapped around her mug, with his. "Too hard for you to hold the teacups now?"

"It's hard to bend my fingers comfortably, but also the warmth feels good when I hold the bigger mug. A little arthritis, that's all. One of the non-perks of getting old."

"There are perks?"

She laughed. "Too many to count. Not the least of which is seeing my grandson safe after months of my being too scared to sleep."

"I'm sorry. I'm here now, though. I hope you slept last night."

"It was easier. For Keri, too, I imagine."

"She said as much."

"We sure do like her."

"I hear the feeling is mutual."

"So, when's the wedding?"

He'd been waiting for the question. "When we're ready."

"I hope it's before that baby comes. You don't want to be the first in our family to have a child out of wedlock, do you?"

"Do you have a new hairstyle?"

She shook a finger at his diversionary tactic, then patted the soft, silvery curls. "As a matter of fact, I do. Dixie fixed it this morning. Do you like it?"

"Very hip."

She laughed. "Hip? Me? Well, that's…awesome."

Jake laughed then, too. He looked around to see if Keri was nearby before he spoke again. "She's going to want to use your Geo. I'd appreciate it if you wouldn't let her."

"Why would she do that?"

"So that she has her own car to drive, but I intend to do the driving until she's not pregnant anymore." And beyond. He wanted a sturdy car for his baby to ride in. But that was an argument for later.

"Honey, she hasn't driven for a month. She said she was too close to the steering wheel to be safe. The girl walks everywhere. Said she'd have an easier delivery and recovery if she did."

Jake sat back. If that were the case, why had she made a big deal out of her wanting the car?

When Keri was ready to go, she came in to hug Nana Mae. “I’m so glad Dixie’s going to stay with you.”

“Well, you know I’m perfectly capable of—”

“It’s going to be so helpful for her,” Keri interrupted smoothly. “Cutting a full four months out of her schooling will be great. That was sweet of you.”

Nana Mae eyed the innocent-looking Keri. “I’ve always liked the girl. I think Joe is crazy to let her slip through his fingers.”

“It’s not over yet,” Keri said, then looked at her watch. “We should get going.”

“Aren’t you forgetting something?” Jake asked.

She looked around, frowning. “I don’t think so, but if I am I can get it later.”

“The car?”

Her cheeks flushed. It was obvious she was deliberately avoiding looking at Nana Mae. “I decided to let you chauffeur me,” Keri said, “since that’s what you want.”

Jake saw his grandmother’s eyebrows arch. She looked from Keri to Jake, her eyes taking on some sparkle. She hid a smile behind a napkin she patted against her lips.

Keri quickly kissed her cheek, apparently wanting to hustle him out of the house before Nana Mae questioned or commented. “Looks like Dixie decided to give you a new look.”

The older woman laughed, then laughed harder. “You two are a match made in heaven, like my William and me. You have interesting times ahead,” she said, then eyed them more thoughtfully. “Will and I didn’t know each other well or for long before we walked down the aisle. Kept things lively for a long time."

Jake carried Keri's filled grocery sacks to the car. He was running out of steam. Too much stimulation without any break, without time alone to assimilate his return to town and independence.

"What did Nana Mae mean?" Keri asked as they headed to the doctor's office.

He could've told her how he'd distracted his grandmother with the same ploy about her hair, too. "You haven't driven her car in a month," he said instead.

"You interrogated her about me?"

"It came up in conversation."

She crossed her arms and faced forward.

"Why did you lie to me?" he asked. When she didn't answer, he pushed. "Keri, now I doubt everything else you've said or will say."

Her foot tapped against the floorboard, but she stayed silent until they pulled into the parking space in front of the doctor's office. He grabbed the door handle, annoyed.

"You left me without transportation," she stated. "And alone."

He turned toward her, not understanding what the big deal was. "So?"

"What if I'd needed to go somewhere?"

"Like where?"

"I don't know." Exasperation strained her voice. "The hospital or something."

"Or something." He pondered that. "If you had an emergency, you would call nine-one-one, right?"

"What if I couldn't?"

He frowned. "Why couldn't you?"

"What if I'd fainted or fallen and couldn't get to a phone?"

Her words hit hard. It was stupid, *selfish,* not to have thought of that. He knew how to deal with bullet wounds, but pregnancy was a mystery. "I'm sorry. It won't happen again."

"And if you're going to leave, please tell me so that I can at least be dropped in town for a while. Your property is beautiful, but it's also fairly remote. I'd rather not be alone there for now."

So much for independence. She was his responsibility now. He wondered if she felt that way about the baby.

He set a hand along her headrest. "How did you feel when you first realized you were pregnant?"

"Shocked." Her gaze met his. "Scared."

"And now?"

"Heart-tied."

"Still scared, though?" he asked.

"Not since you came home."

The weight of responsibility had always sat well on him. He was a man of his word—his honesty, reliability and trustworthiness never questioned. He would fulfill his responsibilities toward his child and Keri, no question.

Just as soon as he figured out exactly what those responsibilities were going to be.

Chapter Six

Keri dangled her legs from the doctor's exam table, trying not to laugh at Jake's reaction to the graphic wall posters representing the stages of pregnancy and child-birth. He slipped his hands into his pockets, toying with something in the left. She'd noticed it before. A lucky coin, maybe? Something small enough not to leave a visible bump, anyway.

Doc Saxon swept into the room. He was no easy-going, rumpled, country doctor as was often portrayed in movies, but a lean, fit, seventy-two-year-old man who maybe looked sixty. Even his thick black hair was shot with very little gray.

"I don't have to ask you how you're doing today,

Miss Keri," he said, taking her hands in both of his. "Those worry lines between your brows are gone."

Keri smiled at Jake. "We are all relieved."

The doctor extended his hand toward Jake. "I'm glad you're home safely."

"Me, too. Thanks."

Without releasing Jake's hand, the doctor moved a little closer. "Don't feel you have to mail me an invitation to the wedding. A phone call will do. Or even an e-mail."

Keri watched the men exchange silent looks. Neither blinked.

"The baby is sitting on my bladder," Keri said into the increasingly tense silence.

"You know where the restroom is," Doc said, turning to her.

"That wasn't my point. I mean this child has dropped as far as it can."

"Getting anxious?" He gestured for her to lie back, then he picked up the fetal Doppler to listen to the heart.

"Anxious to meet our baby." Keri smiled at hearing the heartbeat amplified, a sound that comforted her like little else. She looked at Jake. He moved slowly toward her, as if drawn magnetically to the sound coming out of the speaker.

"Uh, that's a normal rate, right?" he asked the doctor.

"Sure is. Keri's had a problem-free pregnancy."

Jake reached her side just as the doctor put away the monitor, then had her draw up her knees to examine her. She felt Jake's hand wrap around hers, then clench tighter and tighter during the exam.

"Jake." She tried to wriggle her fingers, which were going numb.

"Yeah?" He hadn't taken his eyes off Doc Saxon.

"Look at the ceiling."

He frowned, but he did it—and saw the poster of a cat, claws bared, fur sticking straight out, tail distended and fluffy, eyes wide and wild. RELAX was printed in hot-pink across it.

His grip loosened, but he didn't laugh. Didn't even crack a smile. *What are you thinking, Jake McCoy?*

"Not much change from last week," the doctor said, wheeling his stool back and pulling off his exam gloves. "You can help her sit up, Jake. Any questions?"

"I don't know enough to come up with the questions to ask. Hearing that everything is normal works for me."

"Really?" Doc Saxon looked at him over the top of his glasses. "You don't want to know if you can have sex?"

Keri coughed to cover up the "I do! I do!" that almost came bursting out. Both men stared at her. She coughed again, as if it had only been a tickle in her throat.

"The answer is yes," the doctor said, supplying the answer. "If you're both comfortable with it. I'd advise using a condom to prevent possible infection, if intercourse is what you choose. Intimacy comes in many forms, however. Find what works for you."

Keri tried to appear cool while her hormones were busy doing a happy dance all through her body. "What about orgasm?" she asked, grateful her voice didn't squeak.

"They are good things, in my book," Doc said, straight-faced.

She laughed, because she was supposed to, but she couldn't help but think back to the only one she'd had with Jake, the powerful, almost painfully wonderful one. "I've read that orgasms can be dangerous late in pregnancy. That they can cause the onset of labor."

"You're not far from delivering. It's fine if you end up going into labor anytime. You might as well enjoy it while you can."

Now that the idea was planted, Keri couldn't shake it loose. She wondered if Jake felt the same, or if he was appalled by the idea. She couldn't even look at him, didn't want to try to interpret his expression. He'd just seen her belly naked for the first time, but that wasn't anywhere close to seeing her entire swollen body. Her breasts were huge in comparison to when he saw—*felt*—them last.

"I see I've rendered you both speechless." Doc chuckled. "If you find you have questions, just give me a call. Otherwise, I'll see you next week, same time, or at the hospital. Keep taking your walks, Keri." He leaned toward her. "And I don't care what etiquette experts say, wear a white wedding gown, if you want."

Jake helped her into the car, then held the seat belt while she buckled and adjusted it. She really wanted to know what was on his mind.

"Where to?" he asked, disappointing her.

Short of a discussion about having sex—or better yet, having it—she wanted to take a nap, but she didn't want to force him to stay at home, either. "I could use a little rest. If you'd like to go do something or visit someone, you can leave me at your mom's or grandma's."

"I need some downtime myself."

They headed toward home. "What was it like, growing up here?" she asked. She couldn't imagine staying in one place for an entire childhood. She'd moved six times by the time she turned eighteen.

"Consistent. Full of freedom. We were allowed to roam, once we reached a certain age. Donovan and I went far afield. Joe stayed closer to home. Or maybe not. He's seven years younger. I was gone by the time he got into middle school, so there's a lot about him I don't know. And Donny's four years younger than me, so we didn't pal around a lot, either. We've seen each other quite a bit as adults, however. We occasionally end up in the same country, so we make the effort to meet and hang out."

"Is he your best friend as well as brother?"

"I'd say that, yeah."

How she envied that. Having a sibling as a best friend meant having a best friend for life. Imagine that.

He pointed ahead. "My favorite fishing hole is down that embankment. I practically lived there during the summers. I'd pack a lunch and spend the whole day."

"Alone?"

"No, with friends, eventually girlfriends." He eyed Keri briefly. "Didn't go home with as many trout for dinner from the time I was fourteen or so. Then later, I had a summer job."

"Did you have your first kiss there?"

"Yep."

"What was her name?"

"I can't tell you. She still lives here. You'd see her having lunch at the Lode one day and want to scratch her eyes out."

She laughed. "But you said *girlfriends,* plural. You kissed more than one by your fishing hole. Do they all still live here? Can I travel from house to house and scratch out lots of eyes?"

He gave her a quick, humorous glance. "You know, I don't think I'd put it past you."

"Nah. I don't get jealous."

"Really? I never met anyone who didn't get jealous sometime or other."

She watched him for a minute, enjoying the way he handled the car around the curves, making smooth work of them, a comfortable ride. "Do you get jealous?" she asked.

"Not anymore. But as a teenager and in my twenties? Absolutely."

"Why don't you anymore?"

"Why don't *you?*" he asked as an answer.

"I'm not sure. Maybe because I automatically trust until that person gives me a reason not to. I think a lot of people go at it in reverse. They figure someone has to earn trust. I think that's too hard to do, because the bar keeps getting raised. One misstep can put you back at the bottom."

"Interesting theory." He looked thoughtful as they pulled into his driveway. "I think I don't get jealous anymore because no one's mattered enough."

Including me? "That's harsh."

"I guess it is. Probably shouldn't have said it."

"No. I want you to be honest. Why'd you leave here?" she asked as he turned off the engine.

"There wasn't enough here for me. I needed more than Chance City offered."

"Did you have an idea of what you wanted to do?"

"Not really. I was restless, and I needed to do something. Ended up with a degree in political science, and still didn't know. That's when I joined the army and found a use for my talent for languages."

"And keeping a cool head under fire."

He grinned. "I grew up with seven siblings. I already knew I could do that."

Keri was captivated by his smile, one reflecting good memories. She'd been an only child, with an unspoken wish for siblings and a place to really call home. She'd lived in huts and crumbling houses and sometimes even tents. It was fine, even an adventure, until she was a teenager, then the lack of privacy bothered her a lot. Since earning her nursing degree, she'd only taken jobs where she had her own room in a real house.

"How about you?" Jake asked as they climbed the stairs to his porch. "Why'd you become a nurse?"

"I realized early on that I had a passion for it. Never wanted to do anything else."

"Why do you work in South America?"

"It's where I was offered my first job, which led to another, then another, all by word of mouth."

"You have no accent, no problem with English at all."

"My parents only spoke English at home, and I went to college in Arizona. I've kept up with American popular culture through books and movies. I feel American, even though I lived here only as a baby and through my college years and then these past five months."

They went into the cabin, leaving the screen door open to the pleasant May afternoon.

"When do you think you'll go back to work?" she asked, keeping her tone light, as if his answer wasn't one of the important questions she'd asked since he'd come home.

"I don't have the answer to that yet. A day at a time, okay?" He brushed his hand down her hair. "Do you want to take the bedroom?"

She figured he would sleep longer and better in his own bed. "The couch is comfortable for me." She waited until he'd shut the bedroom door before she let herself react to his brief touch. He'd held her hand at times, but those had been out of necessity or courtesy. This touch was all Jake's doing, prompted by nothing she'd done or needed done.

He was so hard to read. She supposed that was what made him good at the work he did, but it sure did make it frustrating on a personal level.

And now there was the whole issue of sex, which she

hadn't even considered. Well, that wasn't exactly the truth. She'd considered it, but discarded the notion.

But now? Now it was all she could think about.

Jake's cell phone rang, jarring him from a deep sleep. He glanced at the time. He'd been asleep for almost two hours. Groggy, he dragged a hand down his face and said hello.

"We need to talk," Donovan said.

"I'm listening."

"In person. Without Keri."

Jake went on full alert. "I can't leave her here alone."

"I'll see if Mom wants to stay with her while you and I go somewhere and talk. If not Mom, I'll find someone."

"Okay."

Jake cleaned up then went into the living room. Keri was asleep on her side, pillows tucked around her, here and there. He eased closer to her, could see the baby move under her formfitting top. Sleep softened her face, giving her a tranquil look, something he hadn't seen much of, although he knew she'd been trying.

She was holding a lot inside. He could tell by the way she often hesitated before saying something to him.

He wished she would say whatever was on her mind, give it to him with both barrels, as she had the first time they'd met at the Escobar house nine months ago. They'd ended up in an argument. Jake laughed to himself. So much for being able to stay cool under fire.

She'd stood toe-to-toe with him, had riled him up

good. The confrontation had excited him in a way that nothing else had in quite a while. A week later he'd been trying to decide whether to contact her again, when she called to say they were driving to Caracas, that a liver had been found for Escobar and the helicopter hadn't shown up.

She'd been feisty then, too, defiant and protective of her patient—

"What's wrong?"

Lost in the memories, he hadn't seen her wake up. "Donovan's on his way over, and we're going out for a little while. He's bringing someone to stay with you."

"Oh. Okay." She held out a hand to him to help her sit up, shoving throw pillows out of the way, giving herself room, then standing, although wobbling for a moment. "Thanks." She headed off to the bathroom.

Jake went outside and stood on the porch. He was having trouble separating the past from the present, separating the strong, independent, stubborn woman he'd met from the more cooperative, calmer woman of today. Was it the pregnancy that had changed her? Which was the real Keri?

Why did it even matter so much?

Because you liked that strong woman. And you want to sleep with her again.

The voice in his head broadcast the truth. Ever since the doctor had said it was okay to have sex, he'd thought of little beyond that. Or, as Doc said, participating in some other kind of intimacy. Possibilities flashed in vivid neon in his mind.

He wondered how Keri felt about it.

Hell. He felt for the medallion, seeking a means to calm his thoughts. He didn't know why he was even considering sex, given their situation. The only thing he was sure of was that he would always be involved with his child. Where things would end up with Keri was still a question mark. He didn't want to give her false hopes, and surely sleeping together, having sex together, would signal something he didn't mean.

Except that he wanted her, incredible as it seemed, given her condition. If anyone had told him he'd come this close to begging a nine-months-pregnant woman to sleep with him, he would've called that person delusional.

Keri joined him on the porch, not asking where he was going or when he would be back. Did she want to know? Did it matter to her?

Donovan's car came down the driveway. Aggie waved from the passenger seat, probably thrilled to be asked to do something.

Less than a minute later, Jake got into Donovan's car. They didn't drive far, just up the road to a pullout. Donovan turned off the engine.

"A Caracas newspaper ran a story about you today," Donovan said. "Not about the task force, but about Escobar and the kidnapping, and therefore also about you and Keri. It was obvious that Escobar had granted the interview, because he was quoted several times."

Jake clenched his teeth. Donovan had prepared him

for the possibility of a leak to the Venezuelan press, perhaps even to the U.S. media. "Were Keri and I mentioned by name?"

"You, not Keri. But it won't be long before that happens. The journalist who wrote today's story will find more information. I know I would be digging, if I were him."

"So, what happens now, do you think?"

"I contacted my editor at *NewsView*. He's offered me a contract to write the story. It's a good offer, although I might be able to get more. You know I won't write it at all, if you don't want me to. But…"

"Yeah, *but*." Jake thought through the consequences. "Either way, I'm screwed. My name and face will be out there, which will limit my job opportunities. And I'm going to need to get back to work at some point."

"You own a piece of the business. No one's going to fire you."

"I don't want a desk job. I don't want to be the one sending others out to do the jobs."

"I doubt it will be that far reaching, Jake. You could stay out of Venezuela. Or you could even take an alias for work."

Jake considered that for a minute then met his brother's gaze. "Writing this article could be good for your career, I guess?"

"It could ratchet it up a few notches. I've earned a name and reputation already, and this could broaden it. But, I'm telling you, I won't do it if you don't want me to."

"You'd do it right. I have faith in that." As opposed to others who might not be so careful with the details.

"I'd treat it more as an exposé on the kidnapping business in general," Donovan said. "How prevalent it is, how accepted, and the efforts to shut it down. Your story would provide the real example, give it the human touch."

"You'd have to include Keri."

"We'd give her an alias. It's acceptable. No matter what I do, it doesn't mean her name won't be published by someone, somewhere, you know. This story will have hit the wires, and a number of journalists will have jumped on it already. There's something sexy about the dying patient, his nurse and a decorated ex-soldier angle."

Jake crossed his arms and stared straight ahead. "Do the story, Donny. Take the best offer or the best exposure or the best path to a Pulitzer. I'd appreciate it if you tried to keep Keri's name out of it, but I understand that may not be possible. Just stay on top of the news reports and tell me if her name comes up. Marco and the others probably have family and friends willing to even the score for his going to jail."

"That's a small concern, I think, considering he's a proven kidnapper and murderer."

"I know. But she's the mother of my child, and I will protect her. Which reminds me." Jake turned toward his brother. "Why didn't you tell me about her on the drive home?"

He shrugged. "I wanted to see both your reactions. I like Keri, but I also knew she was holding back."

"Did you learn something?"

"Yeah. She was as unhappy to see you as she was happy."

"All that from her expression when I walked in the door?"

"All that."

Jake gave it some thought. He hadn't noticed her at first, so he couldn't gauge her initial reaction. "Did you learn something from *my* expression?"

"Not a thing. You were a blank. Weren't you surprised that she was pregnant?"

"Yeah, I was surprised."

"Unpleasantly?"

"I honestly can't answer that. The fact exists. I can't change anything. I just accepted it."

"*It* being her or her pregnancy?" Donovan asked.

"Both."

"Are you getting married?"

Jake bristled. "Are *you* gonna give me hell about that, too? Of all people, I expected you to understand."

Donovan raised both hands. "Just a simple question. But Keri led us all to believe you and she were in love. And if that's so, why hesitate?"

Jake had to decide whether to confide in his brother or to keep the truth between Keri and himself.

"Look," Donovan said before Jake could answer. "It doesn't matter to me, none of it. I'll support what you do, no matter what it is. You know that."

Jake nodded.

"Is Keri pushing for marriage?"

"No."

"Would she turn you down if you asked?"

"I don't know."

Donovan waited a few beats then said, "You really don't know each other very well, do you?"

Jake paused for just as long. "No. And I feel handcuffed by the family lore that seems to gain momentum as time goes by."

"No babies out of wedlock, and no divorces."

"Right. It's a lot to live up to. And what's the big deal about out of wedlock? There's not much stigma attached to that anymore. Which is worse, do you suppose? That or a divorce?"

"In the eye of the beholder, I think," Donovan said.

"The beholder being Nana Mae."

"Yeah."

Jake rested his arm on the window frame and tapped a rhythmic cadence on the top of the frame. "I always thought the right woman would come along, and I'd know it."

"Hell, Jake, that happened to me, and it still didn't work. The woman's got to feel the same way."

"True." Jake didn't know how Keri felt. She seemed so...pragmatic about it all. So businesslike. Was she as confused as he? Or was she hiding her feelings? He wasn't ready to know the answers to those questions yet.

"By the way, Gideon Falcon wants to talk to you," Donovan said.

"Yeah? Keri told me he got married and is expecting a baby."

"And building a ski resort."

"Amazing. All that happened since I've been gone."

"Time marches on. Speaking of which, I need to get Mom back to town." He started the engine. "So, you're really okay with me writing the article?"

"Write a book, if you want. Or a screenplay."

"Thanks." Donovan made a U-turn onto the highway. "You'll have to tell Mom, and the rest of the family, you know. You don't want them to read about it."

"I will. What's the deal with Joe and Dixie, do you know? You think they broke up for the last time?"

"Neither of them are talking. They secretly watch each other when they're in the same room, so I know there's still a connection there. She broke up with him because he wouldn't set a wedding date. Maybe she's waiting for that this time."

"He seems restless to me," Jake said as they pulled into his driveway. "As much as he's made a success of his business, he doesn't seem satisfied."

"Maybe you can get him to open up. Unlike Mom, who is an open book," Donovan said with a grin when they spotted their mother on the porch gesturing wildly as she talked with Keri. "You know, if you don't marry Keri before the baby comes, Mom's not going to hide her feelings about it."

"Mom's feelings don't make my decisions."

"Yeah, well, good luck with that."

Jake laughed. Aggie McCoy was, indeed, a force to

be reckoned with. Although not as much of one as Maebelle McCoy.

"What do you suppose she had in that big beach bag she brought along with her?" Jake asked as they got out of the car, but then he spotted the answer immediately. A long, pure-white gown was laid over the porch railing, some kind of netting blowing in the wind—and it was way too large to be a christening gown.

"Look what your mother brought," Keri said with forced cheerfulness. "Your sister Carly offered her wedding gown, which should fit since she was also..."

"In the family way," Aggie finished when Keri hesitated. Aggie handed Jake an envelope. "Figured you wouldn't have much time to deal with the details."

Inside was a marriage license.

"It's all filled in, son. You two only need to get someone to perform the ceremony then sign the license. No waiting period. No blood tests."

Silence descended as if a bomb had gone off, leaving nothing alive in its wake. After a good thirty seconds, Donovan took his mother's hand and tugged her down the stairs. "You're due to babysit."

Jake waited until the car disappeared before he looked at Keri.

"I told her I look better in ivory," Keri deadpanned, then her eyes sparkled.

Jake held back a smile. "I imagine she had a solution for that."

"Your cousin Elise has an ivory maternity gown."

"Elise is six-foot-three."

"So Aggie said. But duct tape is the solution to every problem, even hemming."

He landed in the chair next to hers. In his direct line of sight was the wedding gown. He remembered his sister wearing it, her six-months-pregnant belly camouflaged by gathers, the bodice covered in beads—to draw the attention upward, he'd been told.

"I suppose you've dreamed of your wedding all your life, like most girls," he said, having heard his sisters talk about it forever.

"Actually, no. I've dreamed of being a mother, but the whole wedding thing wasn't something that mattered to me."

"You don't want to get married?"

"I didn't say that. I want love and marriage. I just don't need a huge, fancy, costly ceremony. So," she said, her tone a clue to the fact she was changing the subject, "what did you think when you heard the baby's heartbeat?"

He looked right at her. "It made everything real."

Chapter Seven

He was pacing again. Keri sat up in bed the next night listening to him, as she had both nights before. Back and forth, out the front door for a while, back inside. The television was on then off, on then off. She'd had a nightmare for the first time since he'd arrived.

She needed him to hold her. How could she make that happen?

She drummed her fingers on the mattress, considering possibilities. They'd tiptoed around each other all day. She'd caught him looking at her belly—or maybe her whole body—a number of times. He went for walks with her but never held her hand except to help prevent her from stumbling. He also let go quickly, as if afraid to touch her.

She understood that. She was afraid if she put her hands on him, she wouldn't let go, either.

People had called, a few were invited to stop by, each visitor helping to break the tension temporarily, then it would rebuild. She'd gone to bed early and struggled to sleep, only to drift into a nightmare of epic proportions. And now she was awake and shaky from it, listening to him, wishing he would fall asleep himself.

After waiting as long as she could, Keri got out of bed and walked into the living room. She found him sitting on the sofa, wearing a T-shirt and boxers, his elbows resting on his thighs, hands clasped, shoulders slumped. He lifted his head as she neared. She took his hand and pulled him up, then walked back to the bedroom with him, neither of them speaking.

Without letting go of him, she lifted the sheet and climbed under it, tugging him along with her. Resistance emanated from him.

"I had a bad dream," she said as soon as he lay beside her, then she scooted close to him and rested her head against his shoulder.

After a minute, he lifted his arm around her and drew her closer. "Me, too."

She wished he would take off his shirt. She wanted to feel his skin.

"You want to talk about yours?" he asked.

"It's always the same. I'm locked up. It's dark. I can't get out." She slid her arm across his chest. "What about you?"

"Worse."

Tears stung her eyes. She hoped those evil men got the punishment they deserved.

Keri rubbed his chest. He put a hand over hers, stopping the movement, flattening it over his sternum. She recalled that he had some hair on his chest, had pushed up his shirt when they'd made love in their cell. They'd both kept their clothes on, shifting only what was necessary to make intimate contact. And they'd had to be quiet. So very quiet. She remembered biting his shoulder through his shirt as she'd straddled his lap, the feel of his mouth on hers, then on her throat, his tongue trailing down the inside of her arm and on her breasts, the erotic contact of his teeth and tongue on her nipples. She remembered how he felt when he slid inside her, hot and hard, filling her, their mutual orgasms instantaneous and powerful, and how he'd dragged her mouth to his, stopping her moans, tears streaming down her face and into their mouths.

"We're not getting out alive," she'd whispered again and again.

"Yes, we are," he'd whispered back, his voice harsh but sure—

"You're crying," he said now, stopping her memories cold, pulling back to look at her face, the hall light enough to see by. "What's wrong?"

"Do you think about it, Jake?"

"You'll have to be more specific."

"Us, making love in that cell."

Only a blip of hesitation. "Of course I do."

"I can't even believe we did it. That we took that chance. And that we didn't get caught."

"Desperate measures." He settled back against the pillows again and nudged her to lay her head against him. His fingers sifted through her hair.

"I have to tell you something," she whispered. "You don't have to respond, if you don't want to, but I want you to stay here with me all night, even if—"

"Just say it, Keri."

"Ever since the doctor said we could have sex, I've been thinking about it. I feel like I'm on fire all the time. It doesn't matter what you're doing—driving the car or eating or talking to someone else or just sitting on the sofa. I'm all achy and throbbing and—"

He kissed her, a full-out, no-tender-leading-up-to kiss, but with lips and teeth and tongue all involved, on and on and on, as if he couldn't get enough, would never get enough. No one had ever kissed her like that, like she was the sexiest, most desirable woman in the world—and she was nine months pregnant. She never would've guessed she could feel like this. That a man would find her attractive.

The kissing went on until she felt raw, yet she didn't want it to stop. She wanted more, much more. Everything…

Finally he put his hands on her face and held her still. "Do you want to keep going?"

"Yes. Oh, yes."

"What would you like? As Doc said, intimacy comes in many forms. I want you to be comfortable. And sure. And honest, Keri. Please be honest."

She worked up the nerve to be direct. "I want us to

be naked. I want to touch you everywhere. I want to feel your hands on me, all over me. I don't want to hurry, even though I know I won't last long."

He stroked her hair, ran a finger across her lips then kissed her gently.

"Just so you know," she said against his mouth, "my expectations won't change because of this. All it means is I want you. Need you."

"Message received." He touched his forehead to hers and drew a deep breath. "Getting naked was first on your list."

She wore a simple cotton gown that he lifted over her head then laid aside. He didn't touch her, just looked without smiling, without offering words of comfort. Nerves had her shaking. Her body was so different from the last time.

"It's okay," he said softly. "Everything's okay." Then he peeled off his T-shirt and shoved his boxers down and off, kicking them aside.

And, oh, he was glorious in all his naked splendor.

He set his hands on her belly, slid them over her taut skin up to her breasts, across her nipples, then back down again, his touch featherlight. Her internal furnace raged as he sat against the headboard and drew her over him, straddling his thighs, a vivid reminder of their time in the cell—except this time they were naked and assured of privacy. And time. Lots of time.

He leaned forward and ran his tongue over her nipples. She felt an instant tug down the core of her body, where everything tightened and pounded, then when his teeth scraped the hard flesh, she groaned. Reaching for his erection, she wrapped her hand around him, heard him suck in a harsh breath before he moved her hand away.

"Too much," he said. "Too fast."

"Me, too." She set her hands on his chest. "But I need to touch you. To taste you."

He swore, low and harsh. "Just hearing those words…" He held her by the shoulders, struggled for air, his body rigid with resistance.

"So let go and enjoy it," she urged as she took him in both her hands and cherished him. A few seconds later he groaned, then arched, then lost control. His fingers dug into her thighs. She loved the look on his face, the pained ecstasy there. She had done that.

Long moments later he relaxed, limb by limb, muscle by muscle. He opened his eyes and held her gaze as he returned the favor. Straddling him as she was, she was open to him, to his exploring fingers that glided and dipped and aroused. Everywhere he touched added to the fire, the slower and softer the touch, the stronger her response to it. The climax slammed into her without any escalating sensation, only an all-consuming, powerful force that gripped and held and lasted forever, almost too strong to enjoy. She held at the peak, wouldn't go over the top.

"Can't…quite—" she panted "—finish…it."

Jake heard her plea, and the desperation. Was he hurting her? The baby?

"Please, Jake…"

He stuffed pillows under her shoulders and knees, slid down her, settled between her legs, set his mouth on her, slipped his fingers barely inside her. She grabbed his hair and held, then there was no doubt she was finding her own satisfaction.

Finally she went still, and he moved to lie next to her. She opened her eyes, then covered her mouth with her fingers, as if embarrassed. "Did I hurt you? I know I pulled your hair really hard."

"I'm fine." He was more than fine, even though it was probably the dumbest—second dumbest—thing he'd ever done. Now that they'd given in to their needs, how could they go back to what had been? She would expect him to sleep with her from now on. And while he didn't mind that, he figured she would read something into it that wasn't there. Even now she probably wanted the after-sex cuddling that he wasn't good at. "I think I'll take a shower."

He hurried out of the room. While he waited for the water to warm up, he kicked himself for sleeping with her, having sex with her. It wasn't as if she'd forced him, or even rushed him. He'd had plenty of time to walk away.

Jake stepped into the shower. That time they'd made love in the cell had been the same. He could've stopped it at any moment, *should* have stopped it, especially given how it'd turned out. There was something about Keri that made him give in—

"Want your back washed?" the woman being debated asked from outside the glass shower door.

How could he say no? It would hurt her feelings. He'd really painted himself into a corner this time.

He opened the door and held her hand as she stepped inside. Her smile was tentative as she reached around him to grab a bar of soap.

"Turn around," she said.

He did, leaning his hands against the shower wall in front of him, glad not to be facing her or letting her see he was already getting aroused again. What the hell was wrong with him, anyway? He should be protective of her, making sure she was comfortable, not lusting after her, not picturing how she looked when she climaxed.

He closed his eyes and sucked in a breath as she massaged his back with soap-covered hands in long, luxurious strokes, truly massaging him, not just washing. Her fingers eased knots, stretched muscles pliable. How long since someone had done something just for him? A very long time.

You don't let anyone.

The voice in his head spoke the truth, and he was fine with it. He liked being on the move, and every new adventure. He didn't like to be beholden to anyone. He liked doing his job, getting paid and going away, leaving it behind. He wasn't going to be able to do that with Keri—with his child. They were his for life now.

"Am I pushing hard enough?" Keri asked, the heels of her hands pressing into his lower back and dragging down his spine.

"Yeah, it's good." Vulnerable women had always touched off a protective streak in him, but Keri's vulnerability stemmed more from her pregnancy than her personality. In front of the kidnappers she'd held her own, been belligerent, even. It was only when she was alone with him after they'd let Escobar go that she'd shown her fear.

His memories finally shut down as her hands molded his rear, gliding with soapy ease, then her thumbs pushed into pressure points he didn't know he had. He felt her belly brush against him now and then, keeping him mindful of her condition. He should take her back to bed, tuck her in and go sleep on the sofa, let her get some rest.

But the selfish side of him let her continue.

She eased him around to face her and soaped up his chest, taking her time, eventually running her hands over his abdomen until he couldn't hold still any longer. Then she explored him, teased him, tormented him.

"I didn't know if my memories were real," she said, her strokes long and slow.

He sucked in a breath. "In what way?"

"You really are...as I remembered. It wasn't just the heat of the moment."

"You must not have much experience."

She laughed. "I've had few lovers, but I've seen a lot of naked men in the course of my work."

"Aroused?"

"You'd be surprised. It's generally as embarrassing for them as it is for me."

"And some are just flaunting it."

"True."

"Jerks." The thought of it had him clenching his fists. That shouldn't be part of her job. "How do you handle it?"

She laughed, low and sexy. "Interesting choice of words."

"Answer the question."

"If I think it's unintentional, I act as if nothing's happening. If I think they're allowing it, I have someone else come into the room, like their wife or mother. That takes care of it. Generally it doesn't happen twice." She never looked at his face, but kept her head down, her shiny, wet hair reaching her shoulder blades.

He wanted to make love again, more slowly, more thoroughly, so he took control, plucking the bar of soap, reaching around her to wash her back, angling her belly to one side to keep her close. She made purring sounds, the vibration reverberating through him. He knew he couldn't resist much longer….

Hell, it was just one night. Tomorrow things would go back to normal. He would talk to her, make sure she didn't expect a marriage proposal because of this night, make sure she was okay with it. He'd go back to sleeping on the sofa, away from temptation.

Having made his decision, he gave in to that temptation. He switched their positions so that her back would stay warm in the shower, then he soaped her up, top to bottom. She made all the right sounds, all the right movements.

"Let's go back to bed," she said, her fingers pressing hard into his arms.

He turned off the shower and opened the sliding door to reach for the towel.

From behind him he heard her say, “Uh-oh.”

Chapter Eight

Keri met Jake's gaze. "My water just broke," she said, still feeling it trickle.

"Okay. What's next?"

She liked that he didn't show any signs of panic. "I'm going to hang out in here for a little while."

"Do you want me to stay with you or get dressed?"

She clung to his calmness. "Do whatever you want. We're not going anywhere. I haven't had any contractions yet, and they could take hours to start. We won't have to rush off."

"I don't need to call anyone?"

The fact they were having this conversation while they were both naked and had been about to go back to bed and make love again struck her as funny. "Let's not get Aggie all worked up yet."

"I was thinking of Doc Saxon. Believe me, I don't want to call Mom until it's unavoidable."

"Um. Maybe you haven't heard, but she's my labor coach. We took the classes together."

"She's been replaced." He shut the shower door, and she saw the shadowy silhouette of him leaving the room.

"Don't call the doctor yet," Keri shouted, then she turned on the shower and stood under it, her eyes closed, letting the water pour over her. It wasn't what she'd imagined for herself—about to give birth and unmarried—but at least Jake was here with her. If she'd gone into labor three days ago, he wouldn't have been at her side.

After a while she dressed in a fresh nightgown and dried her hair. Jake leaned against the bathroom door jamb the whole time.

"Doc says you should get some sleep while you can," he said when she put the blow-dryer away.

She plunked her fists on her hips. "You called him? I told you not to. He needs sleep, too, you know."

"He made a point of mentioning that." He held out a hand to her.

She didn't have to ask if he would stay with her. She knew he had no intention of leaving her side, no matter how intimately graphic everything got. As a nurse, it didn't bother her. But as a woman who wanted to be seen as desirable, a woman who'd fallen in love—

Jake gripped her arm as she came to a quick stop. She felt the blood drain down her body to her lead feet.

"What's wrong?" he asked, his voice rough.

"Nothing," she answered quickly, making herself move toward the bed again. "I'm just tired."

Fallen in love? No. Not truly. Not deeply. No way. She'd gotten caught up in the town's fantasy of her being in love with him, that's all. And he was the father of her child, about to come into the world. Plus she loved his family and Chance City and the life she'd been building. He'd made love with her, and it was exciting and satisfying.

But it wasn't *love.* That was impossible. She barely knew him.

Keri climbed into bed, content with her conclusion, grateful she'd made sense of it so she could relax instead of brooding about it. He handed her a glass of water, which he'd set on the nightstand. The clock said 2:32. She wasn't the least bit sleepy.

He didn't speak to her, even now as he took the glass when she handed it to him, turned out the light and climbed in bed. She lay on her side, facing him, wondering at his thoughts, because his expression was blank. She couldn't begin to guess what he was feeling and thinking.

"Your mother's going to be very disappointed not to be in the delivery room," she said.

He was lying on his back and spoke to the ceiling. "If you want her there, that's fine. But I'm your coach."

"You don't know what to do."

"Not true. I tracked down your birthing coach yesterday. She condensed your twelve-hour course into two hours for me. I watched videos, asked questions, learned the breathing techniques. I'm prepared."

So, that's where he'd been. Why hadn't he told her yesterday? Why make it a secret? She'd spent that time with Nana Mae, playing Yahtzee.

Keri reached for his hand, deciding maybe he'd kept it a secret as a surprise for her. "Thank you."

"Go to sleep."

She tried, she really did, but sleep was out of her reach. She ran down checklists. The nursery was ready. Her going-to-the-hospital bag was packed. Plenty of food in the refrigerator. Cell phone and iPod charged.

"You're not following doctor's orders," Jake said into the quiet.

She was glad he was awake. He'd been so still, she thought he'd gone to sleep, although she should've known he wouldn't, not unless she did. Maybe not even then. "You didn't tell the doctor we had sex, did you?"

"You think I shouldn't have?"

"Meaning, you did?"

"He *told* us to. Was almost insistent we should..." He let the sentence drift.

"Oh. Right," she muttered. "It's just that it seems like everyone in this town knows everyone's business."

"Small towns are famous for that. But you don't have to worry about Doc Saxon telling anyone, you know."

"I know. I suppose most people either wouldn't believe it or would think we were crazy."

"Crazy horny, maybe."

She smiled. "I guess finishing what we started in the shower is out of the question?"

He didn't say anything, was probably taking her words as a joke, not worthy of comment.

"You really need to sleep, Keri."

"Easy for you to say."

"What would help? What can I do?" he asked.

"Hold me."

"I don't know. That's pretty dangerous. Look what happened last time."

"It was good," she said, not responding to his teasing tone. "Really good."

"Yeah. Roll the other way." He tucked his body along hers, his arms around her, one hand resting on her belly.

She wriggled her backside closer to him.

"Behave yourself," he said.

She laughed softly but closed her eyes, feeling his warmth—too much warmth when added to her own pregnancy furnace—and felt herself drift. She didn't want to fall asleep. Didn't want to give up one second of feeling him wrapped around her. After they'd had sex in the cell, she'd fallen asleep against him, feeling safe for the first time in days, but less than an hour went by before José had come into the cell and quietly helped them escape.

Now José was dead.

"You're not sleeping." Jake's voice rumbled through her.

"I can't stop what's going through my mind."

"Are you worried?"

"Not about the baby. I can't stop thinking about José."

He hugged her tighter, rubbing his chin against her hair, then smoothing it with his hand. "We haven't talked about baby names."

She let him change the subject—it probably wouldn't help to talk about it, anyway. "Do you have some in mind?"

"Maybe. Will he or she have a hyphenated last name?"

"You'd be agreeable to that?"

"Why not?"

"Okay. What are your 'maybe' names?" she asked.

"You first. I'm sure you've been giving it a lot of thought since you've known for much longer."

"Isabella Rachael, after my godmother and mother."

"And if it's a boy? And don't say Jake Jr."

"Sam Jacob. But I'm open to a discussion about them."

He was quiet for a few seconds. "I like Isabella Rachael. But for a boy, I'd rather do Sam Donovan."

"That's fine, Jake. I like it." Although she wondered if it would bother Joe. Maybe there would be a second son someday who they could honor Joe with.

"Good."

She angled back a little to tell him thanks for making it so easy. Her abdomen tightened. She felt it from her back forward. "Did you feel—?"

"You're having a contraction," he said, his hand splayed over her belly.

"Yes. What time is it? We need to time them."

They stayed in bed until the third contraction, each about ten minutes apart. Then she wanted to walk, to help things along. The doctor said not to call until they got down to five minutes. The hospital was only fifteen minutes away.

Jake walked with her, sat with her, let her lean against him. She dozed off and on. He was steady, supportive and…distant, hardly saying anything except to ask her to gauge the intensity of each contraction. He kept track of them, knew in his head how far apart they were and how strong.

Keri turned the responsibility over to him and just let herself live in the moment. She knew that having him with her was an entirely different experience from what it would have been without him. Aggie would've been wonderful, but Jake? He was perfect.

At 11:00 a.m., her contractions had progressed to five minutes apart. They called the doctor, then Aggie and told her to meet them at the hospital, then they headed to the car, stopping on the porch to wait out a contraction, then again right after she climbed in the car.

Keri admired Jake's continued calmness as he walked around the car to the driver's side. He put the key in the ignition, turned it and then didn't put the car in gear but stared out the windshield.

"Jake?"

He didn't answer.

"Jake, what's going on? Why aren't we moving?"

"Something's wrong," he said.

"Everything's fine." A contraction started. She

breathed through it, slow, easy breaths, focusing on a manzanita bush in her line of sight. "Really," she said as it ebbed. "Everything is textbook."

"No. This isn't right."

"What isn't?"

He grabbed her hands. "We have to get married. Now."

Chapter Nine

"Now?" Keri screeched.

Jake had never been more sure of anything in his life. He got it, finally. He understood. He wanted his child born into a marriage, like every other child in the McCoy family. "I'll be right back."

He ran into the cabin, grabbed the envelope with the marriage license and the beach bag stuffed with Carly's wedding dress, and a sport coat for him, then jogged to the car, tossing everything into the backseat.

"How're you doing?" he asked as he headed up the driveway.

"I'm wondering if you've gone crazy," she muttered, arms crossed, resting on her belly.

"You don't want our baby born to parents who are married to each other?"

"I didn't say that. Of course that would be my preference. But you're rushing it, Jake. We hardly know each other."

He gave her a glance before he turned onto the highway, saw the belligerence he'd seen only in the jail. "How many times have you heard about people who've lived together for ten years, then they get married, and within months they're splitting up? I figure we have as good a chance as those people, don't you?"

"So you figure we can get a divorce, no sweat? That we could make a clean break of it?"

"You have a better plan?" He pulled out his cell phone and dialed Donovan.

"Yes," Keri said. "We have the baby and take some time to figure out our future." She closed her eyes and breathed through a contraction.

"I need a favor," Jake said to his brother when he answered. "Give Laura Bannister a call and see if she can line up a judge ASAP, like within the next fifteen minutes, who can come to the hospital and marry Keri and me."

"What changed your—"

"Questions and answers later. Just do it, okay?"

"Consider it done. I'll be in touch."

"You okay?" Jake asked Keri, reaching for her hand.

"The contraction is over, if that's what you're asking. But I'm not okay. You can't just order this wedding, Jake. I'm part of that decision, too."

"So tell me your objections."

"I won't ever want a divorce."

"How do you know that?"

"Because I stick to my commitments," she almost shouted.

He heard the stress in her voice, which quavered with emotion. "I understand and admire that. Look, Keri, no one in my family has been divorced. No one. You think that doesn't put pressure on me, too? I'm putting our child first. I want to be able to say we were married when he or she was born. Lots of marriages don't work out, for lots of different reasons."

"There's no time for a prenup."

He smiled at her ridiculous train of thought. "I'm not after your money."

"I could be after yours."

"No, you're not. And you know I'll always take care of the both of you. I told you that. You can take it to the bank. But if it really matters to you, we can have Laura draw up something in a hurry. I'm sure she's got a basic template—"

"No." Keri blew out a breath then gripped his arm. "Ow. This is a hard one."

Neither of them spoke again until they reached the hospital. Aggie's car was already in the parking lot. Doc Saxon was just pulling in.

"Can you walk, or should I get a wheelchair?" Jake asked Keri as he offered a hand to help her out.

She gave him a look that made him laugh. He felt light-headed. The supersonic pace was at odds with his usual step-by-step way of doing things. But it was the right thing. He knew it.

The doctor came up on Keri's other side.

"You're just in time," Jake said. "You can be a witness at our wedding."

"Won't be the first time," Doc said, then met Jake's gaze. "This is good."

Jake nodded. Yes. It was good.

Keri came to a quick stop at the hospital entrance, and they all waited out her contraction. Then the minute they stepped inside, Aggie raced up and hugged her, then Jake.

"How're you doing?" she asked Keri.

"Just dandy."

Aggie blinked at the sarcasm. She patted Keri's arm. "It'll be over soon, angel," she said, then noticed the bag that Jake carried. Her eyes widened. "Does this mean what I think it means?"

"We're getting married. Would you see if the chapel is available, Mom?"

"You betcha." She eyed Keri with concern. "You don't seem happy about this."

A contraction gripped Keri. Aggie took off to do her task, the doctor went to the OB wing and Jake convinced Keri to sit in a wheelchair while they checked in. A few minutes later, she was in a room being examined and then quickly changing into the wedding gown that fit her surprisingly well. She was wheeled to the chapel, where a judge awaited them, but also Jake's brothers, most of his sisters, Dixie, Laura and Nana Mae.

They raced through the ceremony, cutting to the core

of the vows, borrowed Aggie's wedding ring. Keri looked dazed half the time and in pain the other half. After a brief kiss to commemorate the pronouncement that they were now husband and wife, she was whisked back to the room where she would finish her labor and delivery.

It bothered Jake that Keri stopped talking to him unless he asked a question she had to answer. She looked…hurt. Not just in pain from the labor, but like her feelings were hurt. She rarely made eye contact. His mother gave him questioning looks, which he ignored. Later, when they had privacy, he would get Keri to open up.

After a few more contractions, fierce and close together, the doctor settled on a stool at the foot of the bed. "Let's meet your little one. You can push with the next contraction. Jake, lift her shoulders. Let me know if the mirror needs adjusting for you to see."

Before Jake took his position, he bent close to Keri and whispered, "Thank you for marrying me. It mattered more than I thought." Then he kissed her, a soft press of his lips to hers, longer than the wedding kiss. He felt her quiver, then he backed away and saw a sheen in her eyes, but she said nothing.

After an emotional and physical roller-coaster ride of pushing, their daughter was born, their beautiful Isabella Rachael, who already looked like her mother.

And it took only one glance to understand what Keri had meant by "heart-tied."

* * *

Through a pleasant haze somewhere between sleep and wakefulness, Keri observed what happened around her. Isabella was weighed and measured, cleaned and diapered, then blanketed snugly, a little pink cap on her head pulled down to her eyebrows. Aggie cooed. Jake kept watch, overseeing every step of Isabella's care.

Isabella. Keri had thought for sure she was having a boy. It had taken her a minute to think *daughter* instead of *son*.

Which was only a small adjustment, after all, when weighed against the fact that she was married now. Married to a man whose specialty was damsels in distress.

Is that what changed his mind about marrying her? He thought she needed rescuing? Or had he really only been thinking of the baby, as he said?

She closed her eyes, too tired to think about it. A hand clasped hers. Jake's voice reached her.

"Keri?"

"Hm?"

"A lot of people want to see her. Everyone is still here in the chapel, waiting. Are you up to visitors?"

"I want to hold my daughter first."

He brought Isabella to her, laying her along Keri's side, tucked in her arm. The nurse and Aggie slipped out the door, leaving them alone as a family for the first time.

"How much did she weigh?"

"Seven pounds, seven ounces," Jake answered. "Nineteen inches long. Healthy lungs."

Keri smiled. “I heard.” She ran a finger over Isabella’s tiny face. “I want to see her. Let’s unwrap her.”

“Are you sure?”

Keri pushed the button to raise the back of the hospital bed so that she could sit up. She moved Isabella onto her thighs and opened the blanket. “She’s perfect.” She leaned over to kiss each tiny foot and hand, then bundled her up again when she squirmed, as if ready to wake up. Love poured from Keri to her daughter, a deep, eternal flame. No matter what else happened, they would always have each other.

Keri settled her against her chest. “Where’d the flowers come from?” she asked, spotting a vase of roses.

Jake looked bemused. “That’s the bouquet you carried during the ceremony. You don’t remember? Joe gathered them. Dixie added the ribbon.”

“I don’t remember much about the…wedding.” She still couldn’t believe she was married. In fact, almost everything in her life had been fairly unbelievable since the day she’d met Jake McCoy. “I guess I said ‘I do.’”

“There are witnesses to that effect. When you signed the license, you indicated you were taking my name. Do you remember that?”

“Now that you mention it, yes.”

“If you want to keep Overton, I need to track down the judge before he files the license.”

His tone was level, his face expressionless, and yet somehow she knew it hurt him that she couldn’t remember much. She didn’t want to hurt him. He’d been so good to her since he'd come home, only to find what awaited him. "No, I'm fine with being a McCoy," she said, reaching a hand to him. She already loved his whole family.

And despite the thoughts that had run through her head the night before about it being impossible to love someone that fast, she was pretty sure she did love him. She was just afraid to, wasn't ready to accept or give in to it. She had a feeling she needed to fight it. Unrequited love was too hard.

He sat on the bed and squeezed her hand. "I was proud of you."

Her throat burned. "Thank you. Thank you for being with me all the way. And thank you for my beautiful daughter."

"*Our* beautiful daughter," he said, running a hand down Isabella's back, his hand almost bigger than the bundle she made.

"I never even asked if you like kids."

"Of course I like kids," he said.

The door opened and Aggie stuck her head in. "The natives are getting restless."

"No more than three at a time, Mom," Jake said, standing. "And just for a minute each."

Aggie saluted. "I'll be sure to time them." She grinned and was gone.

"Isabella is very lucky to have Aggie as a grandma. She sure won't see much of her other grandparents, which is really sad to me." Keri wondered what Jake would think of her parents. They were definitely one of a kind.

Joe and Donovan came through the door, Nana Mae between them. And so Isabella met her great-grandmother, her uncles and aunts and good friends Dixie and Laura. She would have a big, loving family, just like Keri had always dreamed of for herself.

She watched Jake hug each person, saw the lifelong connection between them, the comfort of knowing someone all his life, and Keri knew, without a doubt, that she would never leave Chance City.

She'd found home—and it was in a place her brand-new husband didn't call home, even though he'd been born and raised there.

All she needed to do now was find a way to make him feel this was home, too. Because if he couldn't, they didn't stand a chance of their impetuous marriage surviving.

Chapter Ten

Their first argument came on Isabella's one-week birthday.

"You're tired," Jake said as he set a turkey sandwich and glass of milk on a table next to Keri's rocking chair. "You shouldn't be making big decisions yet."

Keri looked up from watching her daughter nurse. He was right about being tired—Isabella demanded to eat every two hours—but it didn't mean Keri wasn't clear minded. "I've been thinking about this for months, Jake. I test drove ten different cars. Now I'm ready to buy."

"I have a car. A solid SUV with a great safety record. Four-wheel drive, should that ever be necessary. A built-in DVD player for when she gets old enough to be entertained. GPS. What more do you want?"

"My own car."

"It doesn't make sense to have two vehicles. When I'm here, I'll drive you. Or you can take the car," he added quickly as she started to protest. "And when I'm gone? Well, that's obvious, isn't it? And at some point, you and Isabella will come on trips with me. We'll expose her to the world. It's perfect. You're used to traveling."

"Which is exactly my point. I've *been* a nomad. I don't want that anymore. I don't want that for my daughter." Keri was trying to stay calm so that Isabella wasn't affected by the increasing stress while she nursed.

"*Our* daughter. And I have a say in this, too." He sat across from her on the sofa, leaning forward intently, his arms on his thighs. "This will always be home base, anyway."

"Are you that anxious to get back to work?"

He looked at her as if she were crazy. "I've spent years building my reputation. To take too much time off would give others a chance to take away business, not just now but in the future. I can't afford that. Which has nothing to do with you getting a car. We don't need two cars."

"You haven't healed enough to go back to work, Jake."

"I think I'm the best judge of that."

Isabella had fallen asleep. Keri started to lift her to her shoulder to burp her when Jake took over.

"Eat your lunch," he said, transferring the baby from Keri's arms to his. "Then sleep."

"Stop ordering me. I know what I need to do. In fact,

why don't you go do something? You've got cabin fever." Dixie had said she might drop by sometime, too, so maybe the women would be able to talk in private. Jake was always around.

Which usually was a good thing, Keri reminded herself.

"I think I'll do that." His mouth was compressed. "But we're not done with this conversation."

So. He was anxious to get out, too. "We are, as far as I'm concerned. And if you won't drive me to the dealership, I'll get someone else to." She heard her own voice rise, ready to do verbal battle with him.

He frowned and walked away. She heard him murmur to Isabella as he laid her in the bassinette in the bedroom, the baby monitor picking up his soothing tone. He'd taken to fatherhood as if he'd had years of experience.

"Last I heard," he said, returning, "marriage involves compromise."

"You telling me what I can and cannot do does not constitute compromise." She took the last bite of her sandwich, as if the discussion weren't bothering her one bit, when, in fact, she hated it. Hated that they were having an argument in the first place, but also that he talked about going back to work, far, far away most of the time.

The car had become a symbol of their separate lives.

"I don't want to fight about this," he said.

"Neither do I. But this much I know, Jake. You're not healed enough to be out on the road again. You still have nightmares." He'd gone back to sleeping on the sofa, but with the baby monitor near him. Whenever Isabella fussed, he was up and in the bedroom, changing her diaper, handing her to Keri, then staying, stretched out on the bed, while she nursed. Keri cherished these moments, learning more about him every day, coming to understand his need for excitement and even danger from the stories he recited about his past.

"I'm better every day," he said, then headed for the front door. "I'm going to track down Joe or Donovan. I'll let you know where I am."

"I have your cell number. Just have fun. Relax. Although you do realize you're leaving me stuck without transportation again?"

He gave her a long, bland look and then left the house.

Keri moved to the sofa and stretched out. She'd no more than closed her eyes when she heard a car coming just after Jake's had left.

She sat up, ran her hands across her face and fluffed her hair. She got to the front door as Dixie came up the stairs, Laura Bannister beside her.

Keri almost groaned. She was comfortable with Dixie, and didn't mind Dixie seeing her exhausted, with a belly like Jell-O and breasts like melons. But Laura was different, an ex-beauty queen turned lawyer who always had her act together. Keri hadn't gotten to know her well, even though Laura had witnessed her fainting at the Lode that first day Keri came to town. Laura had also arranged for the judge to perform the wedding, but other than that, Keri had seen her only a couple of times, and usually at big gatherings.

Not to mention that Dixie and Laura were like the odd couple. So why were they together?

"Jake asked us to keep our visit short because you need to sleep," Dixie said. "We'll only stay a few minutes."

"Asked or told?"

Dixie smiled at Laura. Together they said, "Told."

Keri invited them in. Dixie's stride made her springy, golden-blond curls bounce. Laura glided, her own more ash-blond hair upswept and neat. Perfect. Keri missed her old body and was impatient to have it back.

"Stay as long as you can. I'm fine. Isabella just went down, but she rarely sleeps more than an hour at a time."

"But if you need sleep, we—"

"Please," Keri begged, dragging out the word dramatically. "I need girlfriend time desperately. Help yourself to food. There's iced tea and juice. A whole tray of cookies and brownies are on the counter. Please help me eat them. Jake's not a big sweet eater, and I have no resistance."

Once they were all settled with food and drink, Laura opened a shopping bag she'd brought and pulled out a large, beautifully wrapped package.

"Oh, isn't this pretty! I don't want to open it." Keri peeled the tape carefully, wanting to save the paper to put in Isabella's scrapbook. The box lid sported the name of one of the fanciest shops in Sacramento, the nearest big city, which was where Laura worked in her family-law practice some days and in Chance City the others.

The package held two of the most beautiful baby

dresses Keri had ever seen, along with matching shoes, socks and bows. She felt especially bad now that she hadn't taken the time to get to know Laura, who always seemed alone, even in a big crowd.

Isabella started to fuss. Dixie popped up. "I'll get her, if that's okay."

"Sure. She may need a diaper change, but she can't possibly be hungry yet."

Dixie hurried into the bedroom, leaving Keri alone with Laura.

"Thank you for the beautiful clothes. I can't wait to put them on her. They'll make gorgeous first-photo outfits."

"You're welcome." She was wearing a blue business suit, the skirt just above her knees, and sat with her legs neatly crossed as she sipped iced tea, her very high heels absolutely still.

"Thank you, too, for arranging for Judge Patrick to come to the hospital. We were lucky he was available on such short notice."

"I had fun doing it. And being at your wedding. It's the most spur-of-the-moment ceremony I've attended. You looked beautiful."

Which was such a lie, Keri thought but didn't say out loud. She'd looked like a small whale in a white gown, with deer-in-the-headlights eyes. There wasn't one photo that anyone took—and there were many who'd had digital cameras in hand—that she wanted to frame. "Thank you. The pace was a little…staggering." She listened to Dixie coo at the baby, which made Keri smile. "I'm sorry, Laura. I don't know much about you, except the Chamber of Commerce profile. Do you like splitting your job in two cities?"

"The Sacramento work helps support what I do in Chance City. There's not enough business here to keep me employed full-time."

"You're not married? Have a significant other?"

"I'm not marriage material."

Dixie returned with a fussing Isabella. Jake had discovered that she didn't really like being bundled up tight, as most babies tended to respond to, and because she wasn't wrapped up, she wriggled a lot more, flailing her arms a lot.

Keri saw something in Laura's eyes, a yearning. "Would you like to hold her?" Keri asked.

Laura flattened her hands against her thighs. "Yes, I would."

Dixie transferred her, and Isabella quieted instantly. Keri knew she couldn't see faces clearly yet, but she seemed to look straight into Laura's eyes.

"Oh!" Laura's smile grew broader when Isabella wrapped her hand around Laura's finger. "She's absolutely gorgeous."

Dixie raised her brows at Keri as Laura bent down and kissed Isabella's downy head, her hair pale and surprisingly thick.

"Can I hire you?" Keri asked. "You obviously have the touch."

"She's the first baby I've ever held. That's weird, isn't it? I never babysat as a teenager. Just never felt an affinity for kids, like some people do. I never know what to say to them." She caught Keri's gaze. "Please tell Jake he needs to update his will, and you should, too. Or do a trust. Soon, okay? Now that you've got this precious bundle, you need to make sure she's taken care of."

"I'll tell him. We'll make appointments."

"Very soon," she repeated firmly. "Especially if he's going to continue doing what he was doing."

The thought hadn't even entered Keri's mind. It should have, given that he could've easily been killed at any point in the past five months, even by the people he was supposedly working with.

"Laura, you're scaring her," Dixie said.

"I'm being practical." She passed Isabella to Keri, staring directly into Keri's eyes the whole time, as if she needed to say something but couldn't because of Dixie being there. Or maybe some attorney/client privilege thing that she couldn't say to Keri directly but was willing her to see it for herself. "And with the magazine article having hit the stands today, you know?"

"What magazine article?" Dixie asked.

"The one that Donovan wrote for *NewsView*. The one about the kidnapping."

"What kidnapping?" Dixie asked.

Magazine article? Keri had no idea. How could Laura know something like that when Keri didn't?

Laura crossed the room and picked up the big shopping bag. She pulled out a copy of *NewsView* and passed it to Keri. Jake's photo didn't grace the cover, only a teaser line about a living hell. "Page thirty-five," Laura said. "You aren't mentioned by name."

"You?" Dixie repeated. "Jake did something worthy of Donovan writing about? And you're involved?"

Keri couldn't hold the baby comfortably and open the magazine at the same time while standing. He hadn't told her. Something this important, and he hadn't told her. Had he meant to keep her in the dark? Hoped no one would see it and pass the article on to her? It hadn't taken a day, and she already had it in her hands. He should know that about his town.

"I don't like it when men try to protect me, as if I'm incompetent," Laura said lightly.

Keri nodded agreement, although it wasn't completely the truth. It depended on the situation. She had very much appreciated it when Jake had protected her from the kidnappers.

But this was different.

They all sat. Keri read the article, then Dixie. "What you went through," Dixie said. "I mean, you are the anonymous nurse being referred to, right?"

"Yes."

"And you didn't know the story was going public?"

Keri shook her head. Then it occurred to her… "What if Jake doesn't know? What if Donovan did it on his own?"

Laura laid a hand on her arm. "No way. They're brothers. Wouldn't happen."

A car came down the gravel driveway, a black SUV. Jake was home.

"I think that's our cue," Dixie said, standing. "Call me if you need to talk."

"I will." She focused on Laura. "Thank you."

She nodded, ran her hand over Isabella's head once more and then walked out the door just as Jake reached the top of the porch stairs. He carried a rolled-up magazine in his hand and batted it against his thigh now and then.

Keri couldn't wait to hear what he had to say about it.

Chapter Eleven

Jake was bewildered by the cold-shoulder treatment he got from Laura and Dixie, especially Dixie. Neither of them responded to his greeting. He watched them get into Laura's red Miata and drive off before he went inside the cabin, wondering what he would find. The women had stayed a couple of hours. If nothing else, Keri would be exhausted. Probably not the best time to show her the magazine.

But as he entered the house, he spotted a copy of it on the coffee table.

He set his keys on a table near the front door. "Where's Isabella?"

"I just fed her, and Laura put her to sleep."

"Laura?" The same Laura who had no interest in marriage or children?

"Dix and I are calling her the baby whisperer."

Jake smiled, but he was waiting for the bomb to drop.

"When were you going to tell me about Donovan's article?" Her voice was as cold and controlled as her expression.

"Sometime this week. It wasn't supposed to be published until next week's issue." He sat on the sofa, across from her. "I'm sorry I didn't get to tell you first. It must have been a shock."

"You're sorry you didn't *get* to—" She closed her eyes and gripped the rocking chair arms. "How long have you known about it?"

"About ten days."

"And in all that time, you found no right moment to tell me that my life was about to be turned upside down?"

"In what way? I was named, but you weren't." He wasn't going to be made to feel guilty. He'd protected her as much as he could. So had Donovan. "And a whole lot has happened in the past week, Keri. I wanted to give you time to catch your breath."

Hurt radiated from her. "Every person in this town will know the anonymous nurse was me, Jake. Everyone will know I held back the truth."

"Everyone also loves you."

"Based on a lie." She shoved herself up and paced, gesturing. "Now they'll know we didn't meet and fall in love, that it's all a story. That they were being kind to me under false circumstances."

"I guarantee you, my family won't turn away from you because of this."

"Maybe not. But the relationships will change, become more tentative. Remember when you said you wouldn't trust me to be telling the truth now because I didn't tell you about not driving Nana Mae's car for the past month? Your family and friends will feel the same way about me. I had five months to tell them the truth. I didn't."

He stood, too, and went up to her, cupping her arms with his hands. She tried to pull away, but he needed her to stay there, to listen to him, to believe what he said. "I'll set them straight. I promise."

Frustration emanated from her. "I don't want to set them straight about some things. I'm embarrassed about getting pregnant from a one-night stand. That should've been private and personal."

"You can hardly call it a one-night stand, Keri. There were extenuating circumstances."

"No matter how you clean it up, it was a one-night stand."

She tugged for release, and he let her go. "Maybe technically it was," he said as she walked to the window, keeping her back to him. "But I wanted to sleep with you the day I met you at Escobar's house. It would've happened at some point. And it would've happened more than once."

Jake saw her go rigid. With shock? Disbelief? Revulsion? No, not that, he didn't think.

"Is that the truth?" Her voice barely reached him.

Disbelief. "The day before you called to say that you and Escobar were headed to the hospital, I had already been making plans to see you, rearranging plans I'd made to come home to Chance City, in fact, but detoured to Caracas instead. To see you."

"Why?"

"Because you turned me on like no one I'd met in a very long time. Maybe ever."

A few beats passed. "But I'd ticked you off."

"Yeah. Most people take what I have to say as the truth, based on my expertise. You argued the point that sometimes you would know better than me, based on your own expertise."

"As a nurse, caring for a patient. Not as a kidnapping expert." She faced him. "You were so angry."

"Frustrated—because of your rebel attitude and because I wanted to haul you into the nearest bedroom and spend the next twenty-four hours there with you."

She swallowed. Color flooded her face. Her shoulders dropped some, her defenses relaxing.

"I do apologize for not telling you about the article, Keri. And I will deflect anything negative aimed at you because of it. I think most people will assume we started a relationship before the kidnapping, which is close enough to the truth. They don't need further information, as far as I'm concerned. Does that work for you?"

"Yes. Thank you." Relief softened the muscles around her mouth.

"At the risk of being told I'm ordering you around, I think you should lie down now."

She brushed her hair from her face with her hands. “I must look like a hag.”

“Never.” He could see he’d really thrown her by admitting his attraction for her that first day. She hadn’t reacted in kind, so he guessed she hadn’t felt the same, which surprised him. He was usually a good judge of that sort of thing.

She started to pass by him, but stopped. “Are you in danger because of the article? It didn’t mention Chance City, but I figure that’s because Donovan wrote it. Someone else may find out and publish it. Someone might want to avenge Marco.”

“We’re thinking alike, but Donovan and I believe it’s a small risk.” Although enough that he was considering alarming his house as a preventive measure. “I’m more in danger of losing work because of visibility and recognition. And maybe more because of screwing things up, getting kidnapped myself. It could harm the business. The grapevine will pass it along, just as the grapevine is what gets me and my company business to begin with. Most clients have been satisfied with what I’ve done in the past, so I’m hoping it won’t make much difference. I may have to talk them down a little.”

“Like you’ll have to with your family.”

He nodded. “Please go sleep for a while, Keri.”

“Okay.”

She looked like she could use a hug. They’d barely touched since they came home from the hospital, just what contact came as a result of passing Isabella to each other. He would think about that and what he could do.

But first he had to do a little damage control, make sure his—*their* family and friends didn't think she'd been lying to them, even if she had. It mattered to her, so he needed to take care of it.

He'd start with his mother.

Keri climbed in bed later that night after feeding her daughter and handing her off to Jake. It might only be nine o'clock, but it was dark, and that was good enough for her. Isabella had actually waited two and a half hours between wanting to eat. Progress. Maybe they'd make it to those four-hours-apart feedings that everyone seemed to think were ideal. She sure could use it.

Jake wasn't getting any more sleep than she was, and he seemed to be doing fine. Of course, his body hadn't been put through labor and delivery.

She didn't know if he was still having nightmares, since he was sleeping on the sofa these days. He spent his time taking care of her and the baby, not even letting his mother or sisters help out, which annoyed them, especially Aggie, who wanted to swoop in and take over. She'd been relegated to visitor status.

Jake padded into the room with the baby and put her in the bassinette. Then he stripped down to his boxers and got into bed with her.

"I'm going to start sleeping with you," he said. "That couch is getting smaller every night."

Memories of the first time they'd met had been assaulting her all day, ever since he'd revealed he'd been attracted to her from the beginning. That had come as a total surprise. She remembered having strong feelings about him, too, but she'd identified them as extreme annoyance, not sexual attraction. Maybe they were both. *Probably* they were both.

"I'm glad you're here. You should be comfortable," she said now, sliding over, making room. She tended to sprawl and take up the whole bed when it was just her. "Do you still have nightmares?"

"Yeah. You?"

They were both lying on their backs, talking toward the ceiling. "I don't think I've even had a dream since Isabella was born."

"Maybe you could use a breast pump now and then. Let me feed her with a bottle so that you could get enough sleep to dream."

"That's a good thought, thanks."

Silence settled between them, then without warning tears welled up and began to spill over. A sob escaped her.

He rose up on an elbow. "What's wrong?"

"Nobody called," she said, trying not to break down. "Or came over."

"When?"

"Today."

"Dixie and Laura were here," he said.

"Since then. Since the magazine came out." She looked up at him, barely visible in the dark. "Doesn't that tell you a lot? They've all read the article and have come to their own conclusions. I have to rebuild all that trust that they gave me automatically at the beginning."

He gathered her close. She clung to him, grateful to

be held, grateful to hold on. He ran his hand down her hair and back with long, soothing strokes.

"Not everyone trusted you, if that helps," he said. "You earned trust, and you will again—if it's even an issue."

"Someone didn't trust me?" she said, her voice notching up a level. "Who?"

Jake laughed softly. He wasn't about to tell her that Donovan had been suspicious from day one. Others may say the same thing now that the real story was out. "I knew there was something about that girl," someone was bound to comment, wanting to be right.

"Who?" she repeated. "Who didn't trust me?"

Isabella made a little sound—not the one she made when she was gearing up to cry, but something different.

"Shh," he whispered to Keri. "Let's see if she'll stay asleep."

Keri went silent—for a few seconds. "It was Donovan, wasn't it? Oh, he kept that cool, calm surface he's famous for, but I could tell he didn't like me."

"He likes you fine." He shifted her into a more comfortable position, one in which they could both fall asleep and not cause the other to cramp up. "Sleep."

Less than thirty seconds later she was asleep—which attested to her state of exhaustion, if it could beat out her worries about not being trusted. And he, the man who never cuddled, held her until he fell asleep himself, then was still holding her when Isabella demanded to eat later, waking them up. After changing her diaper, he handed her over to Keri, watching as their daughter latched on with fervor.

"You could sleep, you know," Keri said, brushing Isabella's hair over and over with her fingers. "I'll have to get up when she's done anyway. You might as well take advantage of the break."

"I'm fine." He liked watching them. It soothed him as much as it seemed to soothe mother and daughter.

She laid her hand against his face. "I'm glad you're here."

"Me, too." At some point in the past week he'd given up his anger, something he'd needed at the beginning to sustain him through what had happened to him. He'd been blindsided with her pregnancy, but how could anyone justify being openly angry at a woman pregnant with his child? Impossible, at least to him.

It crossed his mind that if he'd decided just one day earlier to go back to Caracas to see her, none of this would've happened. He would've taken charge of Escobar's transport to the hospital. Escobar and Keri wouldn't have been kidnapped. Therefore he wouldn't have been kidnapped. He and Keri wouldn't have had frantic sex in the cell.

They would've had sex at some point—that wouldn't change—but he would've had condoms. Everything would've turned out differently. If only…

He slipped his finger into Isabella's fist. She squeezed it rhythmically, in the same cadence as she nursed.

"What are you thinking about?" Keri asked.

"How beautiful she is." He looked at Keri, then tucked her hair behind her ear so that he could see her face in the darkened room.

"No regrets?" she asked.

"I never have regrets. Things are what they are, as the cliché goes. And how could I regret this?" he said, bending to kiss his daughter's head. She let go of his finger and flattened her hand on Keri's breast, pushing and patting.

"You must have some feelings about everything that's happened."

"Must I?" He smiled at her. "How about you? Any regrets?"

"More curiosity than regrets. What ifs."

Since he'd just been thinking pretty much the same thing, he said nothing. "I'm planning to see Mom in the morning, get things straight with her, then make the rounds to Nana Mae and Joe."

"I'd like to go, too."

"That's fine. Before we go, we'll talk about what we think they should know and what we want to keep to ourselves."

When Isabella was back in her bassinette, Jake closed his eyes, not wanting to talk, wanting Keri to sleep. He drifted…

The nightmare struck full force, as it did most nights. He fought the images in his head. Then a calm voice reached him, rousing him slowly, drawing him out of that world and back into the dark, quiet reality of where he was, and who he was with.

The soft, warm woman in bed with him wrapped him close. He buried his face against her shoulder, took comfort from her.

"Sleep," she whispered, putting her arms around him. "You're safe."

It should bother him, her seeing him powerless like that, and maybe in the morning it would. But for now he accepted what she offered, finding the sleep he needed and the peace he craved.

Chapter Twelve

Aggie was seated in her front porch rocking chair when they pulled up the next morning. It was Isabella's first outing. Aggie was so excited to have her visit that it was hard to gauge her reaction to Keri and Jake, whom she pretty much ignored. Keri thought it was most telling that Aggie didn't hug either of them.

Aggie exclaimed over the baby, lifting her out of the carrier and sitting in the rocker again. Isabella was awake, her face scrunched as she sought the source of the enthusiastic voice.

"Aren't you the most precious little girl in the world. How much you've grown in a couple of days," Aggie cooed. "You look just like your daddy when he was a baby."

Keri exchanged a look with Jake. Everyone said Isabella looked just like her. Was she persona non grata now? No longer welcome?

Her heart sinking, she sat with Jake on the porch swing. He held her hand. She saw Aggie spot the gesture, too, probably more noticeable because they hadn't held hands in public, except during the wedding.

"How are you feeling, Keri?" she asked, jarring Keri with its formality. Aggie usually called her "angel."

"Grumpy. Sleepy. Happy. Sometimes a strange combination of all three."

"Three dwarfs in one," Jake said, smiling at her, encouragement and support in his eyes.

"I was glad you talked to me about what to expect after the birth, Aggie. It's helped a lot."

The awkwardness stretched into a long silence. Aggie rocked Isabella, whose eyes drifted shut. Aggie finally looked up from admiring her granddaughter and said, "So. I guess you didn't think I could handle the truth. I've lived sixty-seven years, experienced plenty of heartache in my time and handled it without falling apart. Yet neither of you thought I should know what was going on. Can you imagine how it feels that you don't trust me? It's a sad, sad day for me."

Jake squeezed Keri's hand when she started to speak. "Be specific, Mom. What's bothering you the most?"

"You, young man—" She stopped for a few seconds, her voice trembling. "I knew what you did carried a certain element of danger. It didn't surprise me that you chose the work you do, because you were always the biggest risk taker in the family. There wasn't a dare your siblings threw at you that you didn't accept. But I didn't know it was so terribly, terribly dangerous." Fear gleamed in her eyes. "Jake. How could you do that? Go undercover like that?"

"I do what I'm good at. And I like it. It feeds my need for excitement."

Keri didn't sigh but she wanted to. It was what she feared most. He would never quit. He needed the adrenaline rush, the self-satisfaction, even the independence. She didn't stand a chance against all that.

"But you're married now," Aggie said. "You have a child."

"It's my job, Mom. So, what else bothers you?"

She shifted her gaze to Keri. "If you'd told me the truth, I could've helped you. Mama said you had nightmares, that she heard you in the night. Talking about it would've helped."

"She was protecting me," Jake said, again squeezing her hand.

"From what?"

"I didn't know what, Aggie," Keri said. "I just knew I had to keep his secrets until he came home."

"How long would you have done that?" Aggie lifted Isabella to her shoulder and rubbed her back as she stirred.

"I don't know. As long as I thought it was necessary. I probably would've talked to Donovan about it, let him help me make a decision."

Aggie's mouth set hard. "Donny's been in the line of fire more times than I can count. For what? A story?

Some prizewinning photos? His kind of thrills. And Jake's is more dangerous than his! How did your father and I raise two such daredevils? And how do I get you to stop?"

"You can't," Keri answered before Jake did. "You have to let them do what makes them happy." She felt his gaze on her, then he lifted her hand and kissed it. She would have decisions to make herself about what made *her* happy. Until then she would enjoy the time with him, not fight with him. He was doing the best he could.

She'd done the same thing for her parents, who needed to do what they did. It was why she was at peace with them, when she could've easily felt ignored instead of loved. They did love her, wholeheartedly. They just didn't show it in the ways that some parents did—like Aggie. And maybe it had made Keri a lot more independent than she might have been otherwise, which wasn't a bad thing at all.

"My mom called this morning," she said to Aggie, changing the subject completely, grateful that things seemed to be okay between them two of them. "They'll be here in three weeks."

"Tell them I want them to stay with me. I've got this big ol' house with plenty of room."

The invitation didn't surprise Keri. Aggie was one of the most generous people she'd ever met. "That's very thoughtful of you."

"Curiosity, plain and simple." She grinned. "We'll be linked for the rest of our lives. I have a need to know them."

"I'm grateful, too," Jake said. "Thanks, Mom. Really big thanks."

Keri laughed. She could only imagine Jake being stuck under the same roof with her parents. They did take a little getting used to.

"Is this a private party or can anyone crash it?" Donovan asked, coming up the porch steps.

"Were your ears burning?" Aggie asked.

"Talking about me, huh? Will you still make me cherry pies, Mom?" He kissed her cheek, then crouched to look at Isabella, who'd woken up but wasn't crying, which was rare. "She looks just like you, Keri."

Keri and Jake laughed.

"Inside joke, I guess," he said, standing.

"Want to hold her?" Jake offered.

"Maybe later. Like in a couple of years."

"It's easier than you think," Jake said, taking Isabella from his mother and planting her in Donovan's arms before he could escape. Isabella puckered up and cried.

"See? It's not that I don't like babies. They don't like me." He shoved her toward Jake then brushed off his hands. "Any coffee made, Mom?"

"There's a full carafe on the counter."

"Can I get anyone else some?" Donovan held the screen door open, waiting for an answer.

"No, thanks," Keri said. "But I'm going to nurse Isabella, so if that makes you squeamish..."

"I figure you're the kind to do a good job of covering up during the process, so I'm good with it." He headed inside.

Keri raised her voice. "That's true, Donovan. But wait'll you hear her smack her gums while she eats. She's a noisy little piglet."

"Hey, Jake," came the quick response. "Mom told me she needed the hose on the washing machine replaced. That's sounds like a two-man job to me."

"Chicken," Jake called back, but he got up and went inside to help his brother avoid the whole nursing-the-baby process.

"And not ashamed of it," Donovan shouted.

Keri loved having brothers-in-law. And sisters-in-law. And all those other friends and relatives she'd inherited when she got pregnant with Jake McCoy's daughter. The continuity of community was one she'd seen everywhere she'd lived, but she'd never stayed long enough for it to happen to her, except in college, where she *had* made friends she still stayed in touch with.

The brothers came outside when she was done nursing.

"We're going fishing, if you don't mind," Jake said.

"Of course I don't. Have fun."

"Do you want to stay here or go home?"

Keri looked at Aggie. "Do you have anything planned?"

"Free as a bird."

"Then I'll stay here. Leave the stroller, please."

"I'll pack you boys a lunch," Aggie said, not waiting for a response before she went inside.

"I wonder if she'll make PB and J, like when we were kids," Donovan said.

"And three Oreos. And six apple slices," Jake added as he pulled the stroller out from the car and set it on the porch.

"And a Hershey's Kiss," they said in unison, then grinned.

Keri desperately wished for a history like that with someone.

"You wait here for the lunch," Jake said. "Then I'll pick you up at Joe's. You probably better call and ask if you can use his fishing gear. He's got good stuff. In fact, why don't you see if he can break away and join us. He's the boss, after all." He kissed Isabella's forehead, then Keri on the lips, lingering a little. "See? You should've had faith in Mom," he said quietly. "It'll be the same with everyone else. They won't blame you."

"Maybe if you'd lived the life that I have, you would understand why I was worried. I don't have the lifelong connections that you do, except with my parents."

"I hadn't thought about it like that. Okay. I get it."

She cupped his face. "Have fun. Catch us dinner."

"I'll try."

She watched him hurry off, as happy as a kid. "Could I speak to you for a minute, Donovan?"

He made an instant transition from brother to…what? Journalist? Something. Gone was the fun, anyway.

"Your article was incredible," she said. "Mesmerizing, actually. Even if I hadn't been involved in the events, it would've fascinated me."

"Thanks. Señor Escobar sends his best to you, by the way. He was happy to hear about Isabella."

"Ah. So that's where you were last week."

"Getting the details right."

"I imagine so. I hadn't read anything of yours before. Your use of language is exquisite. You captured all the emotions just right."

"But?"

She wasn't surprised he heard what was beneath her compliments. "*But,* and Jake hasn't said this specifically, I gather you didn't or maybe even still don't trust me."

"It's my nature to be skeptical. It's what makes me good at my job. I know Jake, and some of the things you said didn't jibe."

"Like what?"

"Like practicing safe sex. That's a priority for him. Yet you got pregnant."

So, Jake hadn't told him how that came to happen. She was grateful for that. "I didn't set out to trap him."

"I wasn't accusing you. But I know he couldn't have been aware you were pregnant while he was undercover because he either wouldn't have done that job or would've at least told me about you so that I could step in if you needed help."

"No, he didn't know. I came here to tell him."

"You were, what, four months pregnant when you got here? Plenty of time to have contacted him and let him know. Why'd you take so long?" His gaze was direct, looking for truth.

"I didn't realize I was pregnant until I was more than three months along, and then I was so shocked, I wasn't sure what to do. Have you ever been taken against your will? It messes you up, big-time. Your body and mind don't mesh in the same way they used to."

His expression softened. "Actually, I have. I got over it by blocking it. I can see where it would take you more time."

"I'm not even there yet, Donovan. But I'm working on it. So is Jake."

"Do you love him?"

"Here you go," Aggie said, coming onto the porch, carrying a small ice chest.

Donovan gave Keri a "we'll finish this later" look. "What'd you fix us, Mom?"

"Roast beef sandwiches, chocolate chip cookies and grapes."

"And a Hershey's Kiss?"

She smiled, looking pleased that he remembered. "Guess you'll find out."

"You're the best, Mom." He hugged her hard, grabbed the chest and took off, waving to Keri as he went.

Saved by the timely Aggie, Keri thought, relaxing into the swing. *Do you love him?* The question consumed Keri. Yes, she loved Jake. It had happened without conscious thought. But could she stay in love with him if he didn't offer love in return? She didn't have the answer to that.

She knew she was being entirely too pragmatic, probably because she was afraid he could hurt her more than anyone ever had, maybe everyone combined, but she was a realist, after all, not a romantic.

Or maybe she'd never let the romantic in her come out to play.

Maybe it was time to find out.

Chapter Thirteen

Three weeks later, Keri's parents came to town. Jake was amazed that two large suitcases and two carry-on bags held all of Rachael and Isaac Overton's worldly possessions. Jake traveled light when he was working, but he had a house and *things*. It was hard to imagine a person's entire life fitting into a suitcase and a carry-on.

Maybe Keri had arrived in Chance City with that little, too. Maybe most of what she owned now, she'd bought recently.

"Have you ever been to this part of the country?" Jake asked Isaac as they started the winding-road part of the trip, close to home.

"Years ago. We protested the war here, in some big open field. We were kids, not even old enough to drink.

Legally," he added with a grin. "Came up in buses from the Haight. When was that, Rach? Sixty-eight? Sixty-nine?"

"July of sixty-nine," Rachael said from the backseat, where she sat with Keri, Isabella in her car seat between them. "You had an attack of appendicitis."

"That's right! We hitchhiked to the hospital, then had to thumb our way back to the Haight when they let me out."

Keri had told—warned?—Jake that her parents, both sixty, were earthy and outspoken. Rachael was a beautiful woman, her hair a silver waterfall down her back, her makeup-free face almost devoid of wrinkles. She was as slender as her daughter, and wore loose, comfortable clothing.

Isaac was just as thin as Rachael. His jeans were old and worn, his Birkenstock sandals also showing signs of wear. His colorful shirt was probably Peruvian, his hair almost as long as his wife's, although more salt-and-pepper. There was a gracefulness to both of them that Jake saw in Keri, day to day. And an absolute joy for life.

Maybe little physical baggage meant little personal baggage, as well.

Jake glanced in the rearview mirror at Keri as she talked with her mom, both of them smiling and chattering without letup, each of them holding one of Isabella's hands.

Rachael touched Keri's throat. "I haven't seen you without your medallion since we gave it to you."

"I know." She rubbed the hollow in her throat. "I've been heartsick about it. I lost it in Venezuela."

Isaac started talking again, preventing Jake from hearing the backseat conversation any longer. Guilt wrapped around him. Her chain had broken, and he'd found it and the medallion in the cell and put it in his pocket, deciding that if they ever got out, he would have it repaired and return it to her.

It'd been an excuse to see her again.

Yet it was still in his pocket, transferred every day to a new pocket, used frequently as his touchstone. He would give it back. Just not yet.

He glanced again in his mirror, catching her eye this time, seeing her smile. She looked more relaxed and happy than he'd seen her in weeks. Sleep came in longer stretches now that their daughter had settled into a more predictable eating schedule. During the night, they often got six straight hours. For the most part, life was peaceful.

It was making him antsy to do something.

Jake took his time getting his in-laws to his mother's house, stopping occasionally to show off the stunning countryside, tracking down the field where they'd done their war protest, which was now a housing complex some fifteen years old, greatly disappointing Isaac.

They drove through downtown Chance City, with its two blocks of quaint shops, including the Take a Lode Off Diner, a women's clothing consignment shop he thought Rachael might be interested in and a store that sold crafts, books and toys—one-stop family shopping.

"I don't have any spare time," Isaac said when Jake asked what he did when he wasn't working. "We teach people how to use their land well, how to become more self-sustaining, and important health issues. It's a twenty-four/seven job. Plus we're often learning a new language. If we have downtime, we rest."

"Will you ever retire?"

"What for? What to?" He glanced back at Rachael. "You want to retire, dearie?"

"Heavens, no. I wouldn't mind having cots to sleep on, however. My bones aren't happy with mats on the floor anymore. That would be the height of luxury."

Aggie was waiting on her front porch when they pulled up. She hurried down the stairs, swept them both into big hugs and made friends for life. Jake stood with Keri, watching as their parents disappeared into the house, leaving their children behind, although Aggie took their mutual granddaughter, car seat, diaper bag and all.

"When will Isabella need to eat again?" Aggie asked on her way up the stairs.

"In a couple of hours," Keri said.

"Go on a date. I don't want to see you until four o'clock." She disappeared into the house.

After a moment of staring at the closed door, Jake met Keri's startled gaze. They'd never been on a date. Did one date one's wife? It was too late for lunch, too early for dinner. Didn't a date involve eating?

"I'd love to see your famous fishing hole," Keri said.

Problem solved. Obviously she'd seen his dilemma

about what to do and was smart enough to make a suggestion rather than wait for him to stumble onto an idea.

"First impression?" Keri asked as they drove off.

"You're going to be beautiful at sixty."

Her face lit up. He supposed he didn't compliment her enough. They'd both been so focused on the baby—no, that was a poor excuse, a convenient one. He wasn't generally one to compliment.

"They're just as you described them," he added. "They have an enviable closeness."

"You think so? I sometimes wonder if they're too close," she said, looking out the side window at the scenery. "Anyway, by tomorrow they'll be anxious to get on their way."

He couldn't see her expression, but he heard the matter-of-factness in her voice, adding to his sense that she'd thought about her parents' situation for a long time. "But they're staying until Saturday, right? The big party?"

"Oh, yes, I'm sure they will. I don't think I've ever been to a party that celebrated so many events at once." She ticked off a list with her fingers. "Our wedding. Isabella's birth. Christmas-in-June for you. My parents coming to town."

"So many occasions. So many gifts."

"I can't imagine where we'll put much more stuff."

Jake parked in a pullout and grabbed a blanket from the back. They hadn't planned for this adventure, so neither of them was dressed for the hike down to the river. He was wearing jeans, fine for a trip to the airport but too warm for the June day outdoors. She had on a cotton shirt and cropped pants—he'd finally learned the term for those—but sandals. He held her hand so she wouldn't slip, then he didn't let go until they were settled at the base of an enormous oak tree within sight of the quick-running river, icy cold from the Sierra snow melt. When he fished, he stayed along at the river's edge. But when he wanted to be alone with his thoughts, this was his favorite spot, a little isolated and private.

"I can see why you love it here so much," she said, taking in the vista. "The river's loud, but I can still hear birds. Everything is so fresh and green."

He'd stopped paying attention to his surroundings when he was a teenager. Back then, getting the girl was more important. But since he'd come home, he'd hiked down to the river several times and found a new appreciation for its beauty.

"If you'd like to nap," he said, "you can put your head in my lap."

"No, thanks. I don't want to waste time sleeping. It's nice having grown-up time, don't you think?" She slipped her arm under his and tucked herself close, resting her head against his shoulder.

Tiny bolts of lightning struck him everywhere at once, especially where her breast pressed against his arm. He saw her breasts several times a day when she nursed, and although it was supposed to be one of the most natural, unsexy things in the world, that wasn't his response, especially when she finished nursing and didn't cover up until after he took Isabella from her. He could've picked up the baby without touching Keri, but he didn't, and he was pretty sure Keri enjoyed the contact, too. Her breasts were softer right after nursing, her nipples often still erect. It took every bit of his control not to run his tongue over them each time.

At the vivid memories, Jake shifted a little, his jeans becoming uncomfortable. Grown-up time, she'd said. Yeah. It was time for some grown-up activity.

"C'mere," he said, taking her hand and helping maneuver her to straddle him.

Her smile was soft and knowing as she wriggled herself into place on the bulge behind his fly. Maybe this had been her plan when she'd suggested coming here. If so, he could kiss her for it. Would definitely kiss her for it. Right now…

Shadows of leaves played on her face. He tunneled his fingers through her hair, cupped her head and drew her near, feeling her quake when their lips met. She sighed into his mouth, wrapped her arms around him and gave herself to the kiss, hot and wet and endless, her hair making a curtain around his face, brushing his skin like flames, her body gliding against him.

He slid his hands down her back, molded her rear, helped her keep the rhythm.

"How much privacy do we have here?" she whispered against his mouth, kissing him at the same time, her tongue hot and busy.

"Depends on what you want to do."

She pulled back just enough to come nose to nose

with him. "I don't think I'm ready for the full deal, but I really want to do something for you."

"I can wait." *Idiot. Take her up on her offer.* "I wouldn't feel right, when you can't."

"Idiot," she said, as if reading his thoughts, although she smiled. "You're being way too gallant. And if you think I don't get something out of pleasing you, you're crazy."

His gaze never leaving hers, he started unbuttoning her blouse. "I need to do something first."

"Okay." The word came out breathless. She wrapped her hands around his wrists but not in a way meant to stop him.

Underneath her blouse she wore a sturdy nursing bra. He reached around her, unhooked it and pushed it up.

"I may leak all over you," she said quietly but not tentatively. Nor did she blush.

"I'll take my chances." He slid his gaze down. Her nipples were hard and inviting. "I get to see you like this a lot, but I don't get to touch." He ran his thumbs over and around her nipples.

She drew a quick breath. "You have my permission to touch anytime you want."

"Can I do this, too?" He put his tongue where his thumbs had been, around and over, not settling his mouth there as he wanted to, but savoring the contours and textures.

"Yes. Oh, yes. Anytime." She moaned softly, her head tipping back. She started to move against him again. He didn't want her to, didn't want to lose control himself, so he slipped his hand between them and cupped her, pressing into her until a long, low moan started deep in her throat and built. He kissed her, wanting to taste her as she found satisfaction, wanting to feel her mouth go slack as she lost touch with reality.

She'd barely finished, hadn't even taken any time to savor the sensations herself, when she slid down his thighs, unzipped his jeans, freed him and put her mouth on him, startling him with wet heat and slick motion. He wanted it to last forever, an impossible wish, given the long buildup the past weeks. His control lasted only seconds, but the end result rocked him with its power, branded itself in his brain.

After a while she sat up and fell against him. "Amazing."

He tightened his hold on her. "You took the word right out of my brain."

"You're going to need to go home and change before we go to your mom's. I don't think my parents will even notice, but Aggie will."

"She won't say anything."

"I'll have a hard time looking at her. I know she'll wink." Keri groaned. "My thighs are killing me." She moved off him, then straightened her clothes as he did his. Before she fastened the last button on her blouse, he pressed a kiss to her skin between her breasts.

She sighed. "One of these days we may actually get to have real sex."

"I know I've done a lot of fantasizing lately, but that seemed plenty real to me."

"You know what I mean. Both of us naked. You inside me."

Oh, yeah. He wanted that, too. "Do you plan to tempt me mercilessly until the doctor gives the okay for that?"

"If I tempt you, I create problems for myself, too."

"So then I repeat, do you plan to tempt me until then?"

"Probably." She ran a finger across his lips. "Feel free to tempt in return."

"I may do that." He looped an arm around her and pulled her close. "I needed this."

"Me, too."

They lingered for another half hour, not talking much, but his was mind busy. Yes, they'd both needed this time together, which had confirmed once again that sex was good between them. No problems or issues there. He'd even gotten used to cuddling in bed, not minding when she hogged the space, almost pushing him out, or when she draped herself over him so that he couldn't move without waking her up. What sex they had was good. He was adjusting to living with her. They didn't argue.

So, why did he get the feeling it wasn't enough? That something critical was missing?

Her medallion seemed to burn guiltily in his pocket. But he just wasn't ready to give it up.

Chapter Fourteen

Jake couldn't count the number of people who showed up for the party, held in the largest park in town. Every picnic table groaned from the weight of the food. Joe and Donovan were manning two barbecues—nothing fancy, just hamburgers and hot dogs. But the salads and desserts would show off the culinary talents of many in the community.

Staying upwind of the barbecue smoke, Jake took a sip of the beer Joe passed him and watched Keri as she made the rounds with her parents, introducing them. She knew people he didn't. A lot of people. He could name the ones who'd been around forever, like his family had, but there were new faces—or kids who had grown up and he no longer recognized them.

Donovan leaned toward him. “I don’t know half these people.”

“I was just thinking the same thing. Yet look at Keri. She doesn’t stumble on anyone’s name. You know everyone here, Joe?”

Joe flipped a couple of burgers then scanned the crowd. “Pretty much.”

His gaze stuck somewhere to the left. Jake followed his line of sight, spotting Dixie with a group of women, all of them laughing, even Laura.

“When did Laura and Dixie become friends?” Jake asked. “They don’t seem like a match.”

“Don’t you remember?” Joe said. “The bachelorette party for Valerie, David Falcon’s wife? Dullest bachelor party since the dawn of time, then the girls showed up at the Stompin’ Grounds and everything got better.”

“You and Dix weren’t speaking then, as I recall.”

“I was being stupid, as usual.”

“If I’ve got the sequence right in my head, you’d asked her to marry you not too long before that.”

“A closed chapter now,” Joe said as he flipped more burgers.

It was no closed chapter. Donovan was right. Joe and Dixie were always sneaking looks at each other.

“So, Donny, you and Laura have been giving each other the eye, I’ve noticed,” Joe said, shifting the focus from himself.

Donovan immediately began moving hot dogs around on his grill. “No way.”

“Why not? She’s just your type,” Jake said. “Not

interested in marriage, career minded. Blonde. Built. You can't say you've never noticed."

"I'm not dead." Donovan took a long sip of beer. "Hey, who's the guy Keri's talking to?"

Jake spotted Keri, saw that her parents were sitting at a table with his mother, who held a sleeping Isabella, and that Keri was talking animatedly with a tall, dark, overly attentive stranger who angled close, never lost eye contact and occasionally touched her arm.

And she seemed to be fine with it.

"Know who that is, Joe?" Jake asked, slipping his hand in his pocket, fingering the medallion.

"Nope. Sorry. Never saw him before." He slid a glance toward Jake. "You know, you might consider buying her a wedding ring."

Jake headed toward Keri. Yes, he should have bought her a ring. She'd returned Aggie's before they'd taken Isabella home from the hospital, even though Aggie protested. But Keri said she knew how important it was to Aggie to keep her ring on. Anyway, Keri was the one stalling on that issue, not him, something that annoyed him more every day, but especially when another man was paying such attention to her.

As Jake neared her, he enjoyed the view. She did look exceptionally beautiful today, her hair shimmering in the sunlight, her outfit sporty, showing off how quickly she'd lost the baby weight.

She saw him coming and waved, her smile widening. He slid an arm around her waist.

"This is my husband, Jake McCoy. Jake, this is Mark

Harlen. He's here for the weekend, visiting Doc Saxon, seeing if he'd like to make Chance City his home and take over Doc's practice."

The man's glance slid down toward Keri's left hand. Some small talk ensued, then Jake asked where he was from.

"Chicago. I'm in my final year of residency."

"Big difference between Chicago and this little town in the middle of nowhere."

Keri's brows arched high. "Hardly the middle of nowhere. Sacramento's an hour in one direction, and San Francisco only three. It doesn't even take an hour to get to Lake Tahoe up north. To me, it's a pretty ideal location. You can drive to the Pacific Coast or the Sierras and back, all in a day. Plus," she went on dramatically, "it's so historic. Founded during the gold rush in the 1850s. It's endlessly fascinating to me."

Doc Saxon joined them. "I see you've met Keri and Jake. Hope they've been telling you what a great place this is to live."

"Opinion swings on that," Mark said.

"Well, I see it from a newcomer's point of view, so I think you should listen to me," Keri said with authority.

"Keri's a nurse," Doc said. "She's making noises about coming to work for me a couple of days a week, so this is one of the friendly faces you'd see."

Jake didn't like the look of anticipation on the young doctor's face. "It's been nice meeting you," Jake said, extending his hand, ending the conversation, then hustling Keri away.

"I guess the green haze covering your eyes made you not notice that Dr. Harlen was wearing a wedding band," she said, a sassy lilt to her voice. "His wife had gone off to nurse their baby in private."

"Green haze?"

"And you said you never get jealous." Her smile was full of satisfaction.

Was that it? He was jealous? Well, maybe. But more frustrated than jealous, he decided. Since their "date" two days ago, they'd been driving each other crazy, not hiding their desire, testing limits. He hadn't been put through the sexual wringer like that in a long time. Hadn't been necessary in a long time. He had grown-up relationships with adult women. Teasing wasn't part of it. There was the hunt and chase, of course, but capture came quickly—or not at all.

Maybe the kidnapping had changed him more than he thought. Maybe it had changed his attitude about everything.

Keri nudged him with her hip. "Lighten up. I'm just having fun with you."

He didn't think so. He'd noticed that when she seemed worried about his reaction to something, she'd fall back to acting as if she were kidding.

He'd also noticed something important about her parents—that for all their gregariousness, they weren't very warm people. Jake was so used to everyone in his family hugging hello and goodbye, it was second nature to do so. For all that Isaac and Rachael were all about saving the world, one small community at a time, they didn't reach out and touch much. Rachael had held Isabella only a couple of times, and Isaac only once. They didn't hug Keri, although she sometimes initiated one. Isaac hadn't asked Jake personal questions, not about work or plans for the future. Isaac seemed to have come to his own conclusions and decided Keri was in good hands.

"Mom and Dad are leaving in the morning," Keri said when they reached the barbecues. Her tone was light, but there was something in her voice. A longing?

"I'm sorry."

"I'm used to it. They're all jazzed about starting a new job in a new place. Keeps them young, I guess." She waved at someone ahead. "I hated that part of my childhood. The constant moving."

"And yet that's what you've been doing for the past eight years."

"Ironic, hm? I'm so happy to be planted here." She sighed dramatically.

"You do seem to know the entire community."

"Not really, but I joined the women's club and helped with the pancake breakfast for the fire department. Oh, and I decorated a float for the Founder's Day parade. I was having lunch with Dixie in the Lode one day and Honey was short a waitress, so I volunteered and got to know even more people. I had a blast."

This was all news to him. "Did you waitress when you were in college?"

"Nope. My maiden voyage. I mixed things up and messed things up, and everyone was cool with it. I got great tips, too." She laughed. "Being pregnant helped, I'm sure."

"Sympathy tips."

"I gave it all to Honey. She refused to take it, but she put it on a tab for me, so I've got a few free lunches ahead."

Keri wasn't just involved, Jake realized; she was entrenched.

"So, yeah, I know a lot of people, especially added to the fact there's not a soul in town who Aggie doesn't know, and I hung out with her a whole lot. She took me everywhere, introduced me to everyone." Her voice caught. "She's been more of a mom to me..."

She shook her head, not finishing the sentence. The impact of what she was saying struck Jake with hurricane force. She wanted to stay here, in Chance City, not just when he wasn't on a job, but all the time. He wouldn't see her, or his daughter, except here.

Unless he insisted. Sometimes he stayed in one place for a month or two. He wanted them with him.

"The Falcon family has arrived," she said, waving to the group of eleven crossing the field, thirteen if you counted a couple of pregnancies.

The McCoy brothers had grown up with the Falcon brothers. There'd been friendships and rivalries between them, but most important, history. Jake knew everyone except Gideon's wife, Denise, then realized he'd met her at the famous bachelor/bachelorette party, too. After a few minutes reminiscing about that evening with everyone, Gideon took Jake aside.

"Donovan passed the word that you wanted to talk

to me," Jake said. "I'm sorry I didn't get back to you. Things have been...hectic."

"I understand that, and I would hold off longer if I could, but I've already been waiting six months. I can't put it off."

"Six months? What's on your mind?" Jake asked.

"A job I'm hoping you'll be interested in taking."

"So, does it really hurt as much as they say?" Denise Falcon, Gideon's wife, asked Keri as they waited for their husbands' conversation to end.

"Let me put it this way. You know how they all say you don't remember the pain because you get the big reward for it—the baby? Don't believe it. I remember every second of it."

"I guess that's why it become a woman's war story, to be told again and again."

Keri laughed. "They look intense," she said, gesturing toward their husbands. Similar in height and physique, they talked without laughing, without breaking eye contact much. "Do you know what's going on?'

"Well, since I'm sure Jake will tell you, I'll tease you a little. They're talking about a job."

Keri frowned. She didn't want Jake to leave the country yet. He wasn't healed completely. They hadn't settled enough between them. And she wanted to have real sex with him first. "Soon?"

"As soon as possible, yes. That's all I'll tell you. So, what's the secret to fitting into pre-pregnancy clothes only a month after giving birth? You look amazing."

"Genetics, I think, because I've been eating like a horse, and the only exercise I get is to take Isabella out in the stroller, not the power walks I used to do. Anyway, you haven't seen my belly, which is still a work in progress."

Joe called out that the burgers and hot dogs were on the table, and a humorously competitive rush of people headed toward the feast. Jake and Gideon shook hands, apparently ending their conversation.

"See you shortly, Keri. I'm starved," Denise said, meeting Gideon to get in the long line.

"Ready to eat?" Jake asked.

"Your mom just signaled me that Isabella is hungry. I'll eat after the line thins out."

"How about if I fix you a plate and bring it to you?"

"Thank you. That'd be great."

He turned away.

"Jake? What did Gideon have to say?"

He paused a beat. "He just wanted my advice about something."

Keri waited, but he didn't add anything. "You can't talk about it here?"

"Nothing to talk about. It's no big deal." He strode off, leaving the lie in his wake.

Keri moved toward Nana Mae, who was jostling a crying Isabella. Why had he lied? Keri took a seat next to Nana Mae, tossed a blanket over her shoulder and settled Isabella at her breast. She latched on fiercely, even before her milk had let down completely, making Keri wince.

"She doesn't like being kept waiting, do you, sweet girl?" Keri said as soon as the pain dissolved into a steady suckling.

"She's got her own distinct personality, all right," Nana Mae said. She patted Keri's arm. "What's wrong?"

"I'm just tired." *And my husband wasn't being truthful with me.*

Nana Mae rested her head against the chair, her gaze steady on Keri. "Even under the best circumstances, marriage is a challenge, particularly at the beginning. I figure you two didn't know too much about each other, and you didn't even have time for just *you* before there was Isabella, too. It'll get better."

"I'm sure you're right."

"You say that as if you don't believe it. You have to believe it, dear. Believing is half the battle."

She wanted to, but he wasn't making it easy by lying to her.

"Love is a decision, you know," Nana Mae said.

Keri considered that. "I understand what you mean, but I don't buy it completely. I think staying in love is a decision, but I think falling in love just happens to you. And also, *both* people have to decide they're going to stay in love or it doesn't work, right? It's painful if it's one-sided."

"Is that what's happened? You love and he doesn't?"

Keri clamped her mouth shut. She shouldn't have said anything. She didn't know why she did, except that all those months of living with Nana Mae had brought a certain comfort level. "As you said, it's challenging. We do need time to get to know and understand each other."

The two women sat in companionable silence then while Isabella nursed. Keri even closed her eyes, enjoying the sunny day. She reconsidered Jake's response. Maybe it wasn't that he was lying to her but that he'd decided against taking the job and couldn't talk about it. After all, his work involved top-secret information most of the time that he could never share with her.

Although she couldn't imagine what top-secret job Gideon might have. He and Denise were in the process of building a family recreation resort near Lake Tahoe.

Jake brought plates for Keri and Nana Mae just as Isabella stopped nursing, having fallen asleep. He took their daughter from her with an ease that came from a month of handling her. Keri had taken to motherhood easily. She'd been looking forward to it all her life. But Jake had adapted quickly, too, had changed as many diapers as Keri had.

"Can I get either of you anything else?" he asked, rubbing Isabella's back.

"This is perfect, thanks," Keri said after Nana Mae declined.

"I think I'll see if your parents would like to hold her for a while," he said, giving Keri a wink. "I'll grab the camera, too."

"Looks like a man in love to me," Nana Mae commented.

Looks can be deceiving. He was a man "in like," Keri thought. And he adored his daughter. He and Keri were comfortable together. He was good at defusing potential heated moments coming from differences of opinion. She didn't want to fight, but she wanted more than peaceful coexistence all the time. She wanted to have the most open, honest relationship she'd ever had.

She didn't want him just to like her. He was the kind of man who would stay married because of the children, but Keri didn't want that for herself. She wanted to be loved, completely and forever, not be his obligation.

How much time did she have? How long until he went back to work? He'd been on the phone more and more, talking to his partners, and she could tell he was fired up to do something.

Time had stopped being her friend.

Even the issue of the car had been put on the back burner. That would tell her a lot. If he stopped arguing the point about her getting a car, she would have an answer. It would mean he expected to be around a lot, so that having her own car would be sensible. But if he planned to be gone? One car would do.

In many ways it mattered to her more than a wedding ring, which she'd been holding off on, until she lost all the baby weight—

Which was another lame excuse. She didn't want a ring until it meant something to him, meant *everything* to him. When he talked about driving to Sacramento to look at rings, she always put him off.

And since he hadn't insisted, she didn't figure it mattered much to him.

Chapter Fifteen

"You're good to go."

Doc Saxon's words danced in Keri's head as she left his office two weeks later. Good to go. You can make love with your husband. You can finally have real sex.

Did she want to? The past two weeks had been strained as she waited to see what thc future would bring, the decisions Jake would make. She hadn't even told him when her doctor's appointment was, figuring if he knew, he would have an expectation she wasn't sure she was ready to fulfill.

She also figured he'd checked off the days on his own internal calendar and knew the six-week mark had arrived. He hadn't asked if she'd made an appointment, as if he felt it might be invading her privacy or something.

They'd gone from enjoying each other's company to absolute and constant tension, tiptoeing around anything important. He'd spent more and more time away, hanging out with Donovan and Joe, or on the phone with his partners. He was used to action and was being denied it.

Well, that could change tonight. There could be action galore, if she put to use the items in the gift bag Doc had given her a few minutes ago, which contained a CD called "Pure Romance," a bottle of lubricant that warmed upon use and a box of ribbed condoms.

She'd felt her face heat up when she peeked inside, and he'd laughed.

Yes, she wanted to make love. Even now her body was aching with anticipation. She also needed to find accord with him. But enough to put off her rights as his wife?

In the end, the answer was simple. Some needs trumped others.

When she pulled into the driveway, Jake was sitting on the porch, rocking the baby in the new outdoor rocker her parents had given them before they left. Isabella's eyes were open. She shifted her glance to Keri right away when she spoke, then smiled, her newest skill.

"I'll trade you," Keri said to Jake, passing him Doc's gift bag and taking their daughter from him.

He opened it. He didn't smile, just looked at her, his eyes saying everything.

"He doesn't want me to go on the pill yet," she said, explaining what was perhaps obvious. "And while there's only a small chance of pregnancy at this point, we probably shouldn't take the risk."

"Now?" he asked, his gaze direct and intense.

She wanted him to work for it a little, she decided. Both of them, actually. "Tonight."

"You're a cruel-hearted woman, Keri McCoy," he said, but he did finally smile, as if he would enjoy the whole day of anticipation, too.

In a way it was her wedding night. She'd even bought a sexy negligee last week, worthy of a memory or two—or dare she hope for three?

She smiled to herself. Yes, a girl could always hope.

Timing was everything, Jake thought, when you had a breastfeeding infant in the house. Last night, Isabella had slept from around ten until six in the morning. He and Keri had made the decision to move the baby into the office, now nursery, and were rewarded for their nervousness with a full night's sleep—if one didn't count all the times they woke up and checked on her. In the morning, they'd toasted each other with glasses of orange juice to whomever had invented the baby monitor.

But tonight was different. Jake took a shower while Keri fed Isabella around nine-thirty, then he took over, walking her to sleep and putting her to bed while Keri showered. He wished it was winter so that he could light a fire for ambiance. Instead he stood next to the CD player, and the second she opened the bathroom door he started the music. Personally he would've preferred something other than violins, but at this point he doubted he would even hear it for long.

Keri appeared in the doorway, looking a little tentative—and incredibly hot. She wore a long, red, almost see-through gown, her breasts two tempting mounds above the low-cut bodice. Her nipples were hard, their silhouettes visible. He wore plain black pajama bottoms he'd dug out of a drawer, not remembering why he even owned them, anticipating the moment when she would untie them and let them fall.

She didn't come toward him, so he went to her, took her hand and pulled her along with him into a space he'd cleared in the living room so they could dance.

He took her in his arms and moved with her. "You are so beautiful," he said, her hair drifting down his chest, her warm breath dusting his neck.

She snuggled closer, tucked her head against him. "So are you."

He slid his arms down her back and drew her even closer.

"I think you're happy to see me," she said, her hips moving against him, a smile in her voice.

"I've been happy to see you since the day I met you."

She moved her arms from around his neck, angling back a little to put enough room between them to let her fingers explore his chest, pressing a kiss here and there.

"You smell good," he said, nuzzling her hair.

"You don't like my regular scent? Eau de infant?"

He laughed low. "I like that scent fine. But at the moment, you don't seem like anyone's mother."

He could tell he'd said the right thing. She stopped smiling, her eyes turned dark and full of temptation, her lips opening a little, luscious and in need of kissing....

She tasted like a dream, responded like a fantasy. She spoke about need and want and forever, the words breathless and jumbled. He could've taken her right there, on the floor or on the sofa, but he lifted her and took her to their bedroom as she licked his neck, sending chills all through him.

He'd already folded back the bedding, lit several candles. He couldn't remember ever being this anxious before, wanting to please so much. He was trembling when he set her down next to the bed, cupped her face and kissed her. Her fingers dug into his rear. He'd had some grand notion that he would be able to sustain foreplay, to make it last for a long time.

Foolish notion.

Apparently she had no desire to wait any longer, either, because she moved away slightly, put her fingers on the drawstring of his pajamas and pulled, the whisper of fabric making him suck in a quick breath. The garment pooled at his feet. He let her take the lead—just for the moment….

Keri admired him for several seconds without touching, taking her time to enjoy the sight. "I can't wait to feel you inside me."

He groaned. A second later, her gown had joined his pajamas. She had a passing thought about her not-yet-firm belly then discarded it when he bent to kiss her there, then he moved his hands all over her, a slow, gentle tease from head to toe, as if she'd needed any teasing at all. The second time could be slow. This time she just *needed*.

They moved onto the bed, twined around each other, their hearts beating loud enough to feel each other's, a double rhythm. *I love you.* She wanted to tell him, ached to hear him say the same words. But what she said was, "Hurry."

He didn't keep her waiting. The feel of his hot skin against hers, and the spiraling pleasure of him filling her, caressing her from the inside, was like nothing she'd known. Real sex. Beautiful sex. Making love. Yes, making love, utterly and completely. His arms enveloping her, his body covering and moving in a way that comforted and thrilled until there was no more time to think. Her mind emptied, shattered by the explosion inside her, every color of the rainbow bursting behind her eyes. Then the flattering and satisfying recognition that he had joined her in the celebration.

The wait was over—and worth it.

Jake didn't have words to describe how he felt. He rolled onto his side, taking her with him, pulling her as close as he could. He felt her breath, warm and shaky, against his chest, and her head beneath his chin, her hair soft and fragrant, her skin dewy.

This changes everything.

Maybe everything was too big of a word, but a lot would be different now. He hadn't wanted to care deeply about her before, because he'd known he wouldn't give up his work, and he didn't think he'd ever meet a woman who could adapt to his life—until now. In the end, he hadn't even had to make a decision about if or who. The decision had been made for him that night in a cell in Venezuela, when he'd only sought to comfort her and it had escalated into lovemaking that had resulted in Isabella.

He wouldn't go so far as to say it was meant to be, but he was beginning to believe a little in fate.

He was also ready to get back to work and was grateful they'd found accord with each other in time for him to accept a new assignment. He understood that she loved Chance City, and it would always be their home base, but work and his subsequent fulfillment meant being where the action was.

"Are you awake?" he asked, summoning the strength to speak.

"I took a nap this afternoon for a reason." She sounded drowsy and sexy. "I don't plan to sleep again for a while. Do you?"

She angled back so that he was able to see her expression. "You look just like Isabella after she's eaten," he said, kissing her. "Satisfied."

"For the moment."

He raised his brows.

"I expect you'll find me pretty demanding." She bit lightly into his shoulder, an enticing nip, then launched into a long, sexy commentary in Spanish about what she intended to do to him the rest of the night.

He returned the favor in French.

"I think you just told me how to build a car," she said.

He hadn't, but then he did just that, giving it a sensual lilt and spreading kisses over her at the same time, an apparent promise of more sex but instead talking about axels, transmissions and drive shafts.

"Votre arbre d'unité est très agréable," she said in a singularly sexy voice. *Your drive shaft is very nice.*

He laughed in surprise at her perfect French. "I'm glad you think so. And just how many languages do you speak, Mrs. McCoy?"

"Eight. I learned French in Cameroon."

"So you trump my seven. Why didn't you mention it?"

"To take advantage of a moment like this," she said, grinning.

It was good to see her lighthearted and at ease. He felt the same, although experience had proven that such things often preceded disaster of some kind in his life. He hoped not this time. He wanted this to last.

"Stay put," he said, climbing out of bed. "I'll be right back."

He peeked into Isabella's room, the hall light just enough to see her. He gently rested his hand on her chest, feeling it rise and fall. Her lower lip moved as if nursing. He didn't have to guess what she was dreaming about. He would probably have a similar dream himself tonight.

Smiling, he headed into the kitchen, grabbed a box from the refrigerator that he'd told Keri she couldn't open, two forks, two wedding-gift crystal flutes and a bottle of sparkling cider he'd hidden in a paper bag. Champagne would've been nice to celebrate the occasion, but he knew Keri—no matter what any expert said, she wouldn't take even a sip of something alcoholic while she was still nursing.

He was surprised to find her exactly where he'd left her. He'd expected her to get up and check on the baby herself, or even just pull the sheet over her, but she was still stretched out, gloriously naked, candlelight flickering over her.

"Are you going to keep your hair long?" he asked, admiring how it flowed over her shoulders, a shiny lock coiling above one breast like an invitation to kiss it.

"I've been debating. I do like being able to clip it out of my way. Do you have a preference?"

"Like this."

"I figured. That's what I'll do. For now."

He laughed. She never let him get the upper hand, and he liked that about her, how she kept him on his toes.

Jake grabbed a bed tray leaning against the nightstand and managed to set everything on it. He opened the cider and poured, passing her one flute. She sat up, started to drag the sheet into her lap. He stopped her, just shook his head and then held up his glass to her.

"To you, and new beginnings," he said.

She looked as if she were going to add something but then tapped her glass to his and took a sip. He wondered, though, what she would've said—and why it was important to him. She wasn't shy. She talked a lot, in fact, but he'd come to realize she kept a lot to herself, too. She spoke about life and the world, but she rarely said how she *felt* about life and the world. Him. Their marriage.

"What's in the box?" she asked.

He lifted the lid and pulled out the pie inside, placing it on the tray.

Her face lit up. “Key lime! My absolute favorite. How did you know?”

“Honey.”

“Oh, and she makes the best.” Keri dove her fork into the pie and took a huge bite, her eyes closing, her expression one of immense pleasure.

Everything about her turned him on. He’d fought it—just a little—but now accepted that fact. Even the way she ate pie.

Keri noticed his response and raised her brows.

“How does it make you to feel, knowing you do that to me so easily?” he asked, scooping up a bite for himself.

“Happy. Relieved. *Powerful,*” she added before she took another bite and savored it in a way that seemed utterly erotic to him. “You have the same effect on me.”

They teased each other a little longer, finally able to take a little time to enjoy the touches and caresses, the curves and planes of each other’s bodies, the hidden and unhidden places that brought instant response and, finally, the same enormous satisfaction.

Life was good.

Chapter Sixteen

Three days had passed since their "wedding night." They'd been insatiable since then, taking advantage of Isabella's naps as well as enjoying the nights. Everyone else had seemed to look at their calendars and left them alone. They hadn't gone anywhere, and no one dropped by, only called, hints of "I know what you've been up to" in their voices. Keri didn't care. She was in love from her head to her toes, and everywhere in between was being satisfied completely.

Then Jake dropped a bomb as they sat down to dinner. "I have to go out of town tomorrow."

Keri's previous contentment shattered into a million fragments. "You're going away?" Her mouth went dry. Her heart thudded.

"It's a short trip," Jake answered, stabbing a piece of chicken and setting Isabella's bouncy chair into motion again when she looked ready to cry. "No more than a week."

"Where?"

"Costa Rica."

A safe enough place. Generally. Nowhere seemed safe to Keri anymore. "What will you be doing?"

"Preliminary plans for a security overhaul for an appliance manufacturer's home and factory."

She'd avoided thinking about him going anywhere. Had almost convinced herself he wouldn't leave, even as she was aware of his pent-up energy and his excitement when he talked to his partners. His head was back in the game, and he was happy. Happy to be sleeping with her, too, but that wasn't his whole life. He needed it all.

He reached across the dining table and took her hand. "Keri?"

"What?"

"I'll come back."

"You'd better."

"You knew this day was coming," he said gently.

Her appetite disappeared. She looked at Isabella, who was smiling as Jake made faces at her. She was so close to laughing for the first time....

What if she laughed while Jake was gone? And how many other firsts would he miss?

"I'm sorry." She pushed away from the table. "I need to go for a walk. Alone, okay?"

He eyed her steadily. "Take your cell phone."

"I will." She grabbed her phone and a couple of tissues, just in case, and headed up the driveway. She walked and walked, until she saw the path down to his favorite fishing hole and detoured there. It was late June, and although it was dinnertime, she had a couple of hours of daylight left.

She recognized the sprawling oak tree from their last visit and decided not to sit there, instead continuing down to the river. She dipped her hand in the water, still cold and running fast. Another couple of months and it should be warm enough to bring Isabella to dangle her feet. What would she think? Would she laugh? Holler? Need her popsicle toes kissed to warm them?

How much time would the two of them spend on their own? Yes, Keri had known this was coming, as Jake reminded her. She'd been worried for weeks. But his leaving hadn't been a reality until he'd voiced the words out loud.

Now she knew how far beyond worried she was.

She was terrified.

He'd helped bring down a kidnapping ring, including the offshoot that had taken *him*. Them. He might have enemies who would pay for information on him. She didn't know if she could ever get used to it.

"Hey! If it isn't my favorite sister-in-law." Donovan trudged toward her, fishing pole in hand, a creel slung over his shoulder.

She made herself smile. "Your only sister-in-law."

"You're quibbling." He stopped short of her and frowned. "You've been crying."

"No, I haven't. I think I'm allergic to something around here."

He crossed his arms. "If you want me to trust you, as you said, you need to be honest with me."

She mirrored his pose. "I don't recall telling you I want you to trust me. I said you *didn't* trust me."

"Splitting hairs." He held up his hands in surrender. "Anyway, I do trust you. And like you. I think you're good for my brother."

"He's leaving." A hot lump in her throat had her swallowing hard and fast.

"Ah."

She studied the landscape that she'd come to love. "Have you ever been in love, Donovan?"

"Yes."

"Why aren't you with her?"

"Anne only loved her career."

"I'm sorry."

"It's been years. I'm long over it. But thanks." He moved downstream a few feet and cast his spinner into the river.

"Jake loves his career," she said to his back.

"You can't compare Jake and Anne. He made a commitment to you and Isabella."

Such as it was, she thought. He married her, yes, but he'd done it for his family, to respect the McCoy traditions. Certainly he was good to her. Kind. Thoughtful.

Passionate.

But she wanted more. She wanted love.

"How'd you get over her?" she asked. "Anne."

"Decided to."

Love is a decision, Nana Mae, too, had said. "It couldn't be that simple."

He pondered that. "Yeah, it was, pretty much. I'm not one to hang on to a useless cause. If it's not working, walk away."

"I don't know if that's sensible or just cold."

"I've been accused of the latter. Doesn't bother me."

"Why have you been hanging around, Donovan? Word is you're never here for more than a few days at a time, like Jake. Although Jake at least owns a cabin. You've been here for almost two months."

"Having fun driving Joe crazy," he said with a grin. "He's used to his peace and quiet."

"You haven't stayed just to drive Joe crazy. I would never buy that."

"To be honest, I don't even know why myself. Guess I was a little burned out. Having Jake here was the key. It's been good reconnecting. I'm about ready to fly the coop, though. Starting to get anxious to go someplace and do something."

"Like Jake."

"When you've honed certain skills and you've earned hard-fought-for credibility, you want to keep at it, you know? Joe, Jake and me? We're not cut out for inactivity. We like to work. We like to be the best at what we do. That's something our mom and dad instilled in us." He turned and gave her a steady look. "Send him off with a smile. It's going to be hard for him, too, but he'll try not to show it. He'll come back, Keri."

"You can't guarantee me that," she said, then she walked away, back to her husband and baby.

They were waiting outside for her. She kissed Isabella, then lifted her head to kiss Jake. "Are you flying out of Sacramento or San Francisco?"

"Sacramento, then connecting in Dallas." He studied her. "Are you okay?"

"I'll be fine."

He stroked her hair, which almost reduced her to mush. "I know it's hard. We've had an idyllic time."

How can it be idyllic when you've never said you love me?

You never told him, either.

Well…that's different.

The snippy dialogue in her head annoyed her. She wanted to send him off with a smile, as Donovan suggested. It made sense to do that—even if it felt like a lie.

"So," she said. "I'll drive you to the airport."

"No need. Donovan said he would. My flight's at six-thirty in the morning."

"You know if we had two cars, you could drive yourself and leave yours there, so you could come and go without having to rely on someone else."

He groaned. "You don't miss an opportunity."

"Funny how often opportunities present themselves."

He tugged her hair as they made their way back into the house. She noticed he'd covered her dinner plate with plastic wrap. She put the plate in the microwave and started it, then grabbed her salad from the refrigerator.

He sat with her while she ate before passing Isabella to her and going off to pack. "Just you and me, kid," she whispered against her daughter's soft, fragrant hair as she rinsed and loaded dishes with one hand, then wiped down the counter. "We'd better get used to it."

She wandered into the bedroom. A well-used leather duffel bag sat on the bed, zipped shut, but no Jake in sight. She found him in Isabella's room, smoothing the crib sheets, straightening the bumper pads, double-checking the Winnie the Pooh mobile's mount, making sure it was secure, then he just stood there, his hands resting on the crib bar, fingers gripping it.

Isabella made a sound, as if talking to him. He spun around, and Keri noted his stark expression. It was going to be hard for him to leave, just as Donovan said.

He reached for the baby, who babbled a string of adorable sounds, making both parents laugh. Isabella did, too. Keri's gaze met Jake's, sharing the precious moment.

"You probably want to get to bed early," she said after a moment.

"I'll sleep on the plane."

"You'll be extra vigilant, right?" she managed to ask.

"I will. Don't worry."

"It's my nature."

He nodded. "You know you could stay at Mom's, if you wanted."

"I'd prefer to be here. We'll have to adjust to it sometime. Might as well be now."

"At some point, on some trips, you'll come along." The words may have been an order, but his tone wasn't. It was more matter-of-fact, as if they'd resolved that issue already, when, in fact, they'd only just begun to talk about it.

"We'll see," Keri said.

His mouth tightened but he made no response.

"What would you like to do tonight?" he asked instead. Isabella wouldn't be ready to eat and go to bed for another couple of hours.

"Let's try to videotape her laughing. We can load it onto your laptop."

"Good idea." He tickled Isabella, and she laughed. "It wasn't a fluke. She's figured it out."

Ready for her close-up, Isabella laughed and babbled. Keri got a lot of footage of father and daughter, both video and stills. While Keri nursed Isabella prior to bedtime, Jake uploaded everything. It was hard to decipher his emotions, but he took his time viewing and sorting the photos.

He finally turned his laptop to face her. "My new screen saver."

Mother and daughter, their cheeks touching, two matching sets of light brown eyes sparkling. "She has your mouth," Keri said, just realizing it. "Your lips."

"She's all you."

Keri shook her head. "You're there, too." Isabella's mouth went slack on Keri's nipple. She'd gone to sleep.

"Now, there's a picture." He didn't snap one with the camera but seemed to burn the image into his brain, his gaze intense.

"I'll take her," he said, cradling Keri's exposed breast first, her nipple pressing into his palm, then sliding to lift Isabella. "Maybe you'd like to shower?"

"Join me?"

"It would be my pleasure."

By the time she'd clipped up her hair and waited for the water to warm enough to step into the spray, he'd climbed into the shower with her. They soaped each other up, delving into crevices, gliding over surfaces, starving for each other.

He didn't let her towel off but picked her up and carried her to their bed, where he licked the drops off her. After she'd climaxed the first time, he rolled with her so that she was on top. She grabbed the headboard for balance. He told her in Spanish how much he loved watching her like this; in French, how he would never forget this moment.

Just as he began to arch, signaling his own rise, she realized he wasn't wearing a condom. She lifted, pulled back. His eyes flew open. His fingers squeezed her hips.

"You didn't put on…forgot…" Her words came out hesitantly. She leaned across him, grabbed the drawer handle of the nightstand, dug for a packet. She fumbled putting it on him, having never done it before. He gritted his teeth, his muscles rock hard, as he waited her out. This was the picture she wanted in her head of him—this barely-in-control, passionate moment. He not only wanted her, he needed her. She would cling to that while he was gone.

She lowered herself onto him again, not moving for several seconds, then finally letting him finish, giving him a memory to keep him warm while they were apart.

Chapter Seventeen

The first Fourth of July celebration Keri experienced was just after her freshman year in college in Phoenix, eleven years ago, a professionally staged production choreographed to patriotic music. Since she hadn't grown up in the United States, she hadn't felt lifelong patriotism until the fireworks filled the sky and the music soared, giving her chills. Her awe had been the perfect excuse for her friends to tease her mercilessly, mimicking her expression to a T, but still, each July, she'd looked forward to repeating the experience, even the teasing, and was never disappointed. She always carried her own small flag to wave.

The Chance City Independence Day festivities would begin with a parade through the historic streets of downtown, followed by a huge celebration of food, games, music, then fireworks at the fairgrounds. Hardly a soul wasn't wearing something with red, white or blue. Kids were sticky with lemonade, and the scent of barbecue wafted through the air. Every table held a watermelon and a pie—apple, more often than not.

Keri let everything happen around her. She was too excited to participate in any of the games, could barely join in the conversations going on around her.

Jake was on his way home.

He'd been gone six days, had called every night. She didn't tell him how hard it was to sleep without him there, how Isabella was different without him there, too. Fussier. Inflicting guilt wasn't something Keri did, not intentionally. He had a job to do. How could he be faulted for that?

But he'd called last night to say he would be home tonight, maybe in time for the fireworks at nine-thirty. She hadn't told his family, wanting them to be surprised.

"Is this seat taken?" Denise Falcon sat without waiting for an answer. "I'm only six months along. It's going to get worse, isn't it? How did you deal with the exhaustion?"

"I haven't."

Denise groaned and laughed.

"I'm not kidding, Denise. You just go from pregnancy exhaustion to new-baby exhaustion, which actually had gotten better, then Jake left on a business trip and sleep has eluded me, not to mention doing everything myself after being completely spoiled by him."

"I can imagine," Denise said, taking a sip of the iced tea she'd brought with her. "I was sorry he didn't take

Gideon up on his offer. I thought the job would be perfect for Jake, especially now that he has a family. I do understand that it would've been a very different life, especially after all he's accomplished. But sometimes our priorities change. I know mine did. When I fell in love with Gideon, my goals did a one-eighty."

Keri didn't want to admit that Jake hadn't confided in her, so she made a noncommittal sound.

"Men sure think differently from us, don't they?" Denise asked, apparently a rhetorical question since she plunged on. "If I'd just had a baby, I sure would've found any way possible to stay home, not be flying all over the world. And Jake gets a job like Gideon's dropped in his lap? But then, he's also built quite a career for himself. Switching gears would be hard."

Wait. What? Keri reran Denise's words. *Gideon offered Jake a job here? In Chance City?*

Keri treaded carefully. "Jake was flattered that Gideon asked."

"Flattered? Well, Gideon had been waiting since December to make the offer, not even knowing then that Jake would have even more reason to live here year-round. My husband doesn't think he'll find anyone else as qualified as Jake to take over his business. How often do you come across someone who can fly helicopters and small planes, knows fishing and hunting and survival techniques? Really, Gideon's been looking since Jake turned him down, and there's been no one qualified enough."

He said Gideon wanted his advice about something. That it was no big deal.

He hadn't even discussed it with her, probably knowing she would've debated the issue with him.

He *had* lied. Her instincts were right. He hadn't trusted her with the truth.

The shock of that, the pain of it, rushed through her, weighting her down.

"Are you okay?" Denise asked, her hand on Keri's arm.

"No. No, I don't feel well. The heat maybe." She just wanted to take her daughter and go home.

Home. He didn't call his cabin home, only a house. But to her—

"You don't look well. Can I drive you home?"

She'd driven to Aggie's and parked there, then pushed Isabella in the stroller. "I've got my car, thanks. Maybe I'll sit for a little while longer. See if it passes. It's just a headache."

"I'll stay with you."

Keri's cell phone rang. She almost didn't pull it out of her pocket, figuring it was Jake and not wanting to talk to him yet, but it was her mother.

"We just arrived, safe and sound," Rachael said.

They'd taken three weeks off, traveling to see friends before settling in for what would probably be a two-year assignment. They'd stayed longer with some friends than they'd stayed in Chance City. Keri fought against the disappointment all over again.

"Did you have a good time, Mom?"

"We had a wonderful time. But I called to tell Jake thank you."

"For what?"

"Didn't he tell you? He arranged for a bed for us! Oh, honey, it's so nice. We were hoping to be provided with cots, but Jake managed to order us a bed, with mosquito netting and really soft sheets and everything. What a sweet thing to do. Our bones thank him, too."

They talked for a few more minutes, but her mother was in hurry to go, was always in a hurry to go.

"My mom," Keri said to Denise when she closed her phone. "She and my dad are in Africa. Jake...did something really nice for them, for their comfort."

"Something that's going to make you cry?"

Keri laughed a little, lied a little. "The headache's doing that. I think I'll go home for a while, try to knock it down before the fireworks later." But she knew she wouldn't be back. She couldn't face him knowing what she knew now, not in front of everyone else. She couldn't fake it that well. "I'm sorry," she said to Denise, then left to get her daughter from Aggie to take her home.

After suggestions for her to just lie down at Aggie's and offers for someone to take her home while another person drove her car for her, she made her escape.

Aggie's disappointment and Nana Mae's concern followed Keri home—figuratively, anyway. Donovan followed her home literally. He got out of his car, unbuckled Isabella and brought her carrier inside.

Keri didn't want to talk to him. She thanked him but didn't offer any refreshments or for him to sit. She needed to think.

"Anything you need to talk about?" he asked.

"No. But thank you."

"Are you going to call Jake and let him know not to meet you at the fairgrounds?"

She turned a sharp gaze on him. "How did you know about that?"

"He told me. I'm picking him up, remember? I didn't tell anyone else." He glanced at Isabella as she started to fuss in her carrier. "You know I'll tell him. I don't want him to be blindsided by your not being there."

"That's your option, I guess." *Go away.*

"Are you mad at him?"

He bought my parents a bed. What other man would think to do that?

"Please, Donovan. Just go. I need to feed the baby." She figured that was the fastest way to get rid of him.

He left, and she gathered Isabella close, sat in the rocker and thought about her future.

Jake waited for Donovan to pull out of the driveway before he headed toward his house. It'd been a good week, a productive week. And the phone call with Keri to end each day was the icing on the cake.

She'd sounded so excited when he said he would be home tonight, then Donovan burst that bubble. She wasn't with his family getting ready to enjoy the fireworks, which would start soon. She claimed she had a headache, but Donny had seen her talking with Denise Falcon right before the "headache" had struck.

Jake figured Denise told Keri about the job. Women

sure did stick together. Laura had told Keri about the magazine article before he'd gotten a chance to. Now Denise had beaten him to it about the job.

So now there was going to be hell to pay. They'd resolved the other issue just fine. He didn't see any reason that this problem wouldn't be fixed, too.

Jake climbed the stairs and crossed the porch. The door was locked, but that was okay. Safe. He slipped his key in the lock, opened the door and stepped inside, into darkness.

Panic struck him. They were gone—

He flipped a light switch. She was there. In the rocking chair. Not rocking.

"Hi," he said, setting down his bag and keys, going up to her. He didn't push his luck by trying to kiss her.

"Isabella's asleep already."

He needed time to adjust to this Keri, this angry or hurt Keri, so he went down the hall and into the nursery. She'd grown, hadn't she? In less than a week. He'd missed her more than he'd imagined possible. Missed the warm bundle she made on his chest, the way she splashed water in her tiny bathtub, her arms and legs always in motion, how she flattened her hand on Keri's breast when she nursed.

Everything. He'd missed everything.

It had also felt damn good to be working again.

Jake left the room, closing the door halfway. It was face-the-music time.

He took a seat across from Keri and waited.

"You lied to me."

Her stark accusation and hard eyes pierced him. "Technically, I withheld information."

Bad move, McCoy. She curled into herself even more, drawing her legs up, wrapping her arms around them.

"I needed to think about it, Keri. I needed to decide whether it's something I would enjoy. That's not a decision I could make with you. It had to be my own."

"Then what are we doing married? I don't get to participate in any decisions? In the end, yes, it would be your choice. But not to even talk it over with me? That's not a partnership. That's a dictatorship."

"That's unfair. It's the only time I haven't consulted you about—"

"Donovan's article?" she interrupted. "Not a peep. I see a pattern here, Jake. One that doesn't bode well for our marriage."

Uncertainty seeped in. "How can I fix it?"

"Here's what I've decided—without your input because, obviously, we get to make our own decisions now. Isabella and I are moving into town."

Shock barreled through him. "No way."

"I'll have to rent until I find the right house to buy, but that's okay. At least I'll be close to people, not isolated, like here."

"But you won't be staying here all the time. You'll come with me on most jobs."

She unfolded herself, planted her feet on the floor. She suddenly looked very much in control, not hurt, not angry. "No, I won't. *We* won't. I lived that nomadic life, Jake. I hated it. This would be even worse because we would be there for much shorter periods of time. How would I spend my days? I wouldn't have family or friends. We'd be waiting for you to have free time for us. And what about when Isabella starts school—or we have another child? Because I want my daughter to have siblings. She deserves to have what you had and I wanted all my life. Something constant, something to count on. Home. I've never had roots. Now I'm planted here. I want to let my garden grow."

"*Our* daughter," he said, everything inside him red-hot.

"What?"

"You called her *your* daughter. She's ours. And maybe you get to make decisions for yourself, but not about her. As her father, I have to work. I get to provide for her."

"What about me?" Keri thumped her chest. "What about my need to work? I'm trained, too. I have skills I don't want to lose." She shoved herself out of the chair, looked around but then didn't go anywhere.

She closed her eyes for a few seconds, noticeably calming herself down. "The first day you brought me here, you said this was a house, not a home. Just a place to come to. A tax deduction! This isn't my house. I didn't buy it or decorate it, but it became my *home* because of the people in it. It's where I felt safe. It's selfish of you to consider only your needs in this family."

He needed to regroup. He'd never had his emotions raked over the coals like this, never been accused of selfishness. He had awards for heroism….

"I'll go," he said, standing.

"What?"

"You and Isabella can stay here. I'll leave."

She said nothing. He looked at her for a clue, but her expression was closed.

"I'll be back tomorrow, though, to see my—our—daughter. You can't keep her from me."

"I wouldn't do that." She took a step toward him. Her voice softened. "Where will you go?"

"To Joe's. I'd like to keep this between you and me for now, if we can. Until we figure out what we're going to do. You know what it'll be like if Mom knows." Or worse, Nana Mae, he thought. He didn't want to tell her he'd failed at something so vitally important. "At this point, no one knows I'm home except Donny. Joe will, of course. Can you pretend for everyone for now?"

"Yes."

That simple yes gave him hope. If she was positive she wanted to end things, she would've hedged a little. At least that's what he was clinging to, that there was room for negotiation.

He pulled out his cell phone, pushed the speed dial for Donovan. "I'll have Donny come get me so you have the car."

"Thank you."

"Hey," he said into the phone. "Would you mind picking me up?"

"At your place?"

"Yeah."

"I'm in the crowd at the fairgrounds. It'll take me a

bit to get to the car, make arrangements for a ride home for Mom and Nana Mae."

"I'll start walking. Maybe I'll beat you home."

"You okay, Jake?"

He glanced at Keri, who had moved to look out the window. The fireworks were starting. The view from his place was about as perfect as it could get, at least for the big, high, overhead-display part of the show. "Sure."

He ended the call, shoved the phone in his pocket and headed for the door, where he'd left his packed bag from the trip. "I'm sorry, Keri. I never meant to hurt you."

"I know. But I need to look out for me, you know? I haven't been doing that, and I need to."

He wanted so badly to pull her into his arms and never let go. She looked small and fragile standing there at the window. He never would've applied the word *fragile* to her before. Even in the cell she'd been all fire and rebellion for the first two days, only giving in to her fears when the threats had escalated on the third day. The day they'd ended up making love, comforting each other, afraid of impending death.

Before and after that moment, she'd been amazing in her strength.

"I'll call you in the morning," he said.

"Jake?"

Had she changed her mind already? He tried to keep hope out of his voice. "What?"

"Thank you for giving my parents a bed. They were thrilled. It was a lovely surprise."

"I was glad to do it." He stepped out into the night

and started walking. Fireworks lit up the night sky, booms and pops and crackles alerting him of more to come. Then a dud. One long trail of light that fizzled—no sound, no starburst. Just…nothing. And the quiet seemed unbearable afterward.

Just like his life.

He was about half a mile from Joe's when Donovan pulled up beside him. He tossed his bag in the backseat and climbed in.

"She kick you out?" Donny asked.

"I volunteered. We're keeping this quiet, Donny. Mom and Nana Mae and the sisters can't know. I want to work everything out."

"No one will hear it from me. You want to talk about it?"

His instinct was to say no. He was embarrassed and hurt, and he didn't want anyone to see that. He also knew he was in over his head this time. "Yeah, thanks. Joe, too. We'll wait until he gets home, okay?"

Joe didn't get home for almost two hours. By then Jake and Donovan had indulged in a couple shots of whiskey chased by tall, cold beers. Half-empty bags of pretzels and chips were scattered across the coffee table, crumbs everywhere.

Joe came in, looked around and said, "Where's mine?"

When his blood-alcohol level caught up to theirs, he kicked back, put his feet on the coffee table and asked the question Jake kept asking himself.

"What the hell happened?"

"I messed up."

"Well, that goes without saying," Joe muttered. "But *how* did you mess up?"

"Treated her like the 'little woman.' Thought I could be the man of the house and make all the decisions."

"There's your mistake," Donovan said. "You have to be willing to let women make all the decisions. Makes for a much happier life. For them, anyway, which can spill into yours, too."

"Says the expert." Joe aimed his beer bottle toward Donovan, then took a long swig.

"Just because I haven't been married doesn't mean I don't know anything about it. I'm a world-class observer, you know."

"Observe me this, Donny," Joe said, his words a little slurred. "Why doesn't a world-class observer such as yourself not see he's going through a midlife crisis?"

Donovan scoffed. "That's crap. I'm thirty-three. I've got seven years to go. What's your excuse?"

"I'm not the one hiding out from life in the very town I ran away from and never looked back."

"What the hell are you talking about? I come back."

"For weddings and funerals."

"And birthdays, when I can. I stayed this time because I haven't had a vacation in twelve years. I was overdue."

Jake tried to keep his eyes open. There was an important discussion going on, but the words weren't sinking in. "Are we still talking about me and my problems?" Jake asked, confused. "I'm in real pain here."

Joe glared at Donovan. "I understand what you're going through, Jake. I know it hurts."

Jake straightened. He set his half-full bottle of beer down. "What happened between you and Dixie over the years doesn't equate. I'm not diminishing your own situation, Joe, but there's a child involved in this one. And a woman who did become my wife."

"Then I guess you'll have to work harder than I did to fix it."

Even in his haze, Jake heard Joe's grief. Why hadn't he and Dixie worked it out this time? How was it different from their other breakups?

Jake looked toward Donovan and saw he was out cold, his beer bottle still clutched in his hand but his fingers loosening. Jake slid it free, gathered the other empties and took them out to the kitchen. Joe was right behind him with the snack bags.

"Maybe I'm not the best one to give you advice, Jake, but it doesn't take a relationship expert to see where you should start. I've come to my own conclusions about how you and Keri ended up together, and—"

"I don't—"

Joe cut him off with a gesture. "You don't have to tell me anything. And if I'm right, what I'm about to say will make sense to you, and you'll consider it. She never had a courtship. Women like courtships. It fills their memory books. Haven't you heard Nana Mae talk about Grandpa Will and how he courted her? How many times has she told that story to us?"

His kid brother was making a whole lot of sense. "Enough that I've got it memorized."

"There you go. But even more important? You need

to figure out how you feel about her. She shouldn't have to settle for anything less than what she wants. Nor should you, for that matter. But Keri in particular. She's been through a lot. I admire her."

"So do I."

"It's a good place to start. Now, let's haul Donny to bed, so I can get to sleep, too, and you can have the couch. One of us has to get up and go to work tomorrow morning."

Chapter Eighteen

Keri heard a car coming down the driveway early the next morning and was annoyed. He'd said he would call. She'd hardly slept and was still in her robe. Isabella was down for her morning nap. Keri had hoped to take a shower before Jake came.

It wasn't Donovan's car, however, but a bright red sports car.

Keri groaned. Laura Bannister. She'd made arrangements to drop off the paperwork for their new trust so Keri and Jake could read it before coming in to the office to sign. Keri had forgotten.

She felt dowdier than usual. Laura was always dressed so perfectly, her hair and makeup flawless.

Oh, well. Keri finger-combed her hair, grateful she'd

brushed her teeth, and opened the door at Laura's knock.

"Oh, no. I'm early, aren't I? It's a bad habit of mine. I'm on my way to my Sacramento office, but I could come back tonight on my way home."

"You're not early. I had kind of a long night. Please come in."

"Isabella's okay?"

"She's great. Would you like some coffee? I just brewed a pot."

"I would love some, thanks." She followed Keri into the kitchen and set a manila envelope on the counter, patting it once. "I'm glad you took my advice and got your estate in order. Most people feel relieved when they've done it, especially when there's a child involved."

"Cream or sugar?" Keri asked.

"A little milk, please. Jake's not home yet, I gather?"

"Not at the moment."

Laura went silent. Keri set her mug on the counter, not looking at the elegant lawyer until it grew uncomfortable not to.

"I'm very good with nuance," Laura said softly. "And I heard all sorts of nuance in your answer. Jake's not home *at the moment.* If he was home he would be aware I was coming and would've been here. If he was still out of the country, you would've said so."

Keri burst into tears. Dixie was her best friend, but she couldn't talk to her, couldn't share with anyone else, either. But Laura was her lawyer. She had to keep everything confidential, didn't she?

"Um, let's go sit down," Laura said, guiding Keri into the living room.

"I'm sorry. I'm not usually one to fall apart," Keri said, embarrassed.

"Maybe it's postpartum depression?"

Keri laughed shakily. "You say that so hopefully."

Laura half smiled. "I'm solution oriented."

Keri wiped her fingers over her cheeks and sniffed, digging into her pocket for a tissue. "I'm in love with my husband."

"And that's a problem because…?"

"He's not in love with me."

Isabella let out a howl. Keri jumped up at the scary sound and raced into the bedroom. Her arms and legs were wildly in motion. Her cry filled the room, echoing, rebounding, ringing painfully loud. Keri checked to see if a diaper tape had gotten stuck to her skin or her onesie was tangled, but she couldn't find any problem. She held Isabella close and bounced with her, whispering soothing words. This wasn't her hungry cry.

"What's wrong?" Laura asked.

"I don't know. Shhh, sweet girl. You're okay. You're okay." But she wasn't okay. She kept howling.

"May I try?" Laura asked tentatively.

Keri transferred her daughter into Laura's arms. Laura murmured, "There, there. You're going to be all right," and the crying stopped. Tears shut down. Peace reigned.

"How do you do that?" Keri asked.

Laura shook her head. "No idea." She lifted the baby onto her shoulder, and Isabella threw up all over her.

"Oh, no!" Keri pressed her hands to her mouth. "Your beautiful suit." She didn't know what to do first—take Isabella or get something to clean what looked like a silk jacket.

Laura was paralyzed, too, the bewilderment and, yes, aversion, on her face saying it all.

"Here. Let me take her." Keri snatched her away and raced to the kitchen to grab paper towels. Laura cleaned up the best she could.

"Please send me your dry-cleaning bill. If it won't come out, I'll pay to replace the suit."

Laura had regrouped, though. "Don't be silly. I'm sure the cleaners can take care of it. Guess we know what was bothering her, hm?"

"Poor thing. That was some tummy ache, hm, sweet girl?"

"Well, I should get going. Let me know when you want to come into the office—or whatever else you need of me." She rubbed Keri's arm for a minute, although the gesture felt tentative, as if she weren't used to comforting. "You didn't have a prenup, but I hope there'll be no need for that to become an issue."

"You and me, both."

"Is it really that bad, Keri?"

"I don't know yet. I said some things last night to him…. It's hard to know in the light of day how he'll feel. This is just between us, right?"

"Give me a dollar and we'll call it lawyer/client privilege."

Keri headed to get her purse.

"I'm kidding," Laura said, laughing. "Yes, of course it's between us."

Keri hugged her. Laura stiffened first then relaxed into it, Isabella snug between them.

"I've never had many girlfriends," Laura said. "I've been making inroads with Dixie, but it's been an uphill battle. She—most women—don't take to me easily. I'm sorry if I'm not sure what to say that doesn't sound lawyerlike."

"You did fine. I hope you'll consider yourself officially my girlfriend."

Her eyes took on some sparkle. "I'd be honored."

The phone rang as Laura was walking out the door. Keri looked at the caller ID, saw it was Jake.

"Hi," she said, glad he couldn't see how horrible she looked.

"Morning. How are you?"

"Isabella's a little off her schedule today, but I'm okay. How about you?"

"Not okay."

She waited but he didn't add anything. She didn't know what to say.

"I'm on my way," he said. "If that's all right. Is she awake?"

"Yes. Um, I haven't showered yet. And she needs a bath."

"I can give her a bath while you shower."

It would seem too homey. Too…normal. But she didn't know how to tell him no. "That'd be okay, I guess. When will you—" She saw Donovan's car pull into the driveway as Laura left. "You're already here."

"If you'd said no, I wouldn't have turned into the driveway. I'll be right there."

She set down the phone, once again wishing she'd been ready for company. She looked so messy and dull. But he'd seen her give birth, after all. She couldn't look worse than that.

She pressed a kiss to Isabella's head. "Daddy's here, Isabella. Daddy's here."

She looked beautiful. He almost kissed her hello and then realized he couldn't. So instead he reached for Isabella, who scrunched up her face as if ready to cry.

"She doesn't recognize me," he said, stunned by the realization.

"Just give her a minute. She will."

He let her stay in Keri's arms but kept eye contact and held her hand. He wanted to see her smile, hear her laugh. He'd watched the videos of her and Keri every night.

"I saw Laura leaving as I drove in," he said, trying not to jump to conclusions about why she'd been there so early in the morning—not a normal time to drop by for a visit.

"She brought papers." Keri gestured to a packet on the kitchen counter.

Jake's throat closed. Papers? Already? He couldn't delay another second.

"Poor Laura. Isabella threw up all over her."

"How'd she take it?" He eased Isabella away from Keri. As soon as she was settled, she smiled at him. His heart turned upside down. She remembered him.

"Surprisingly, Laura hardly batted an eye." Keri cocked her head. "I think she's lonely."

"Seems hard to imagine, but I don't know her well. She graduated with Joe and Dixie, seven years behind me." He watched Keri tuck her hair behind her ears. He couldn't tell if she was nervous or excited or uncomfortable. "You're so beautiful," he said, the words just spilling out.

"She sure is," Keri said, her gaze on their daughter, not seeing that he was looking at his wife.

"You, Keri. You're so beautiful."

"Oh. Well. Thank you." She was flustered. A blush of color dusted her face. "Um, I can fill Isabella's tub before I get in the shower."

"I can manage." It was all he could do to not run his hand down her hair, slip an arm around her and pull her close. He knew he'd missed her. He just hadn't known how much until he got home.

She walked away. The bathroom door clicked shut. Jake set everything up for Isabella's bath. He talked to her the whole time he bathed her, even as he kept an eye on the manila envelope Laura had left. Isabella smiled and laughed and kicked and splashed. He heard the shower come on, then stop later. The hair dryer started when he was carrying Isabella to the nursery to dress her, stopped when he carried her back into the living room.

Anticipation built in him. He had plans for the day. Big, life-changing plans, the results of which depended on Keri.

All he knew for sure was he wasn't going to take the tack that Joe had. Jake wasn't going to give up. Ever.

Keri couldn't stall any longer. She was showered, blow-dried and dressed in new cropped pants and a T-shirt that hugged her curves. Was she dressing to tempt him? Well, she was human. But she intended to stay on task, to hold out for a different relationship, a partnership.

She found Jake and Isabella on the porch. Keri loved to listen to him talk to their daughter, who now seemed enraptured by his voice as he discussed how the seasons would change the scenery, and how he liked spring the best, and that she shouldn't be afraid of the wild animals that passed through, but she shouldn't try to touch them.

Keri pushed open the screen door and joined them.

"Here's Mommy. Doesn't she look pretty?" Jake said, his gaze all encompassing.

Isabella shifted her eyes toward Keri. She tickled Isabella under her chin, a spot that always made her laugh.

"When will she need to eat again?" Jake asked.

"Anytime now. Although I'm not sure what to do, given the tummy problem this morning." She put her hand on Isabella's forehead, then slid it down the side of her face. "She's not feverish. Maybe I should call Aggie and ask what she thinks."

"While you're at it, would you ask if she'll take Isabella for a while? There's someplace I'd like to take you."

Keri locked gazes with him. "I'm not going to be tempted into having sex with you, Jake. We have a lot to settle."

"Tempted? Now *there's* a word."

She would've thought he was feeling smug except that his nerves were much more in evidence, in the way his jaw tightened and how he held his body. "How long is 'a while'?" she asked.

"A few hours."

"More than a while. So, Aggie knows you're home?"

It said a lot about his state of mind that he hadn't factored that in. "No. I didn't want her—or anyone other than Joe and Donny—to know we weren't together. I guess you can drop me off somewhere, take Isabella to her, then come back and get me."

"Subterfuge," Keri said, surprised, but also in the mood for some intrigue. She went inside and called Aggie, who said yes, nurse the baby, and yes, do bring her over.

Jake made himself scarce while Keri nursed, defusing a potentially tense situation. She appreciated his sensitivity and hated that their relationship had come to this. The strain wore her down.

If they didn't work things out, her next step would be to decide to stop loving him—if she could believe Nana Mae's theory, anyway. And Donovan's. Keri wasn't convinced yet that it was possible to make that kind of decision.

Half an hour later they were on the road. They barely

spoke after she asked where they were going, and he said, "You'll see."

"You'll see" became the Sacramento car dealership for the kind of vehicle she'd decided to buy, one of their biggest disagreements.

"What does this mean?" She barely managed to get the words past the hope that swelled in her throat.

He turned off the engine, rested his hands on the steering wheel and looked at her. "It means I'm going to be home a lot more, although gone some, too. You'll need a car of your own."

"Where are you going?"

"Not far, but overnight sometimes."

Keri put a hand to her lips. "You took the job Gideon offered."

"Sort of. How much do you know about his business?"

Her pulse pounded in her ears. "Hardly anything."

"He built an adventure business, guiding mostly executive-type men into the wilderness to fish or hunt, or take a hike that would challenge them. He flies helicopters into pristine ski areas. It's quite lucrative because he targeted a certain market who could afford the cost and craved the challenge."

"It sounds risky."

"There are certain elements of risk, I won't lie to you, but not the criminal kind. These risks are known and prepared for. When Gideon offered the job, that's all he offered, which is why I turned it down. Well, that, and I wasn't ready to give up my own business that I'd worked so hard for. Then I called Gid this morning, and he's turning it over to me completely. I won't report to anyone, although I'll use his new resort office as a home base. We'll work out a deal for that."

"So you'll be home a lot."

"And gone, too, as I said. I'll keep a financial stake in the other business I've built, too, and take a stateside job now and then to keep my hand in it. But with my language skills, I figure I can entice foreigners here for adventure. That's something that will set me apart from others running the same kind of business."

Keri's eyes and throat burned. She was beyond thrilled about his decision, but there was more she needed to hear. She waited for the right words, her hands clenched, her heart filled with expectation.

"My nightmares had stopped," he said. "You know that. You were responsible for it—your optimism, having you to hold during the night. I hadn't had a nightmare in weeks. But last night I did, and it was completely different from the others. Last night it was about you and Isabella, that I couldn't find you, couldn't take care of you. Joe woke me up from it. I was sweating and shaking. And I knew, then. I knew everything."

He opened the glove compartment and took out a small box. "I love you, Keri. I love your spirit and your bravery and your honesty. I love that you stood your ground with me. And I love how you make me feel, in and out of bed. I love that you made me a father when I had no idea I wanted to be one." He opened the box. Inside was a gold band intricately carved with something that looked at first glance like vines. On closer look, they were ropes.

"You're my lifeline," he said, fingering the pattern, then pulling it out of the velvet slot. "I got tired of waiting for you to choose a ring, so I had this made in Costa Rica. If you don't like it—"

"I love it. I love *you*." She stuck out her hand, let him slide it on, ran her fingers through his hair when he bent to kiss her ring finger. "I love you *so much*. I've waited so long to tell you that."

He kissed her, a hard press of lips, his emotions laid bare for her, then he buried his face in her shoulder and squeezed her for a long, long time.

When he leaned back, he framed her face with his hands. "Joe told me I needed to court you, that you'd been denied a courtship. I know that's true, and I plan to make up for it, I promise, but not apart from you. The truth was right there in front of me, Keri. All I had to do was acknowledge it, and then I figured I'd have to convince you."

"I'm convinced." She smiled and leaned to kiss him. "But there's one thing."

Worry settled in his eyes. She set her hands on his chest, felt the strength there, the steady heartbeat, and knew she and her children would be safe and well loved forever.

"Do you feel like you're the one doing all the giving?" she asked. "Making all the compromises? I don't want you to resent me or regret what you're giving up."

"You did enough giving for both of us. It's my turn. And I don't have regrets, remember? I also think we should buy a house in town so you'll be closer to everyone while I'm gone, if that's what you'd like."

Gratitude raced through her. How could so many good things happen at the same time? She overflowed with happiness. "Yes, I would like that very much. There's a house on Poplar I've had my eye on...."

"I've seen it. We'll check it out later today." He angled back and dug into his pocket. "One more thing." He held up a chain in the air, her medallion dangling from it, and told her how he'd found it and had it repaired, all the while intending to give it back. "Then I couldn't. It was a piece of you I kept with me all the time. When I rubbed it, it calmed me or helped me focus to make a decision. But I know you've been missing it."

"I wouldn't mind at all if you kept it." She liked knowing she would go with him everywhere he went. To her it was a graduation gift from her parents. To him, it held an even more emotional meaning. "I never thought I would ever say this, *mi novio,* my sweetheart. I'm so glad I was kidnapped."

He laughed, the sound joyous. "Let's go buy you a car. I have a sudden need to take you home. I didn't think I could go home again, but now it's where I most want to be. Home heals. I didn't understand that before."

And then he kissed her, tenderly, peacefully. For life.

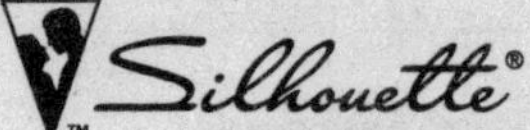

SPECIAL EDITION®

COMING NEXT MONTH

Available September 29, 2009

#1999 THE SHEIK AND THE BOUGHT BRIDE —
Susan Mallery
Famous Families/Desert Rogues
Prince Kateb intended to teach gold digger Victoria McCallen a lesson—he'd make her his mistress to pay off her dad's gambling debt! Until her true colors as a tender, caring woman raised the stakes—and turned the tables on the smitten sheik!

#2000 A WEAVER BABY—Allison Leigh
Men of the Double-C Ranch
Horse trainer J. D. Clay didn't think she could get pregnant—or tha wealthy businessman Jake Forrest could be a loving daddy. But Jak was about to prove her wrong, offering J.D. and their miracle baby love to last a lifetime.

#2001 THE NANNY AND ME—Teresa Southwick
The Nanny Network
Divorce attorney Blake Decker thought *he* had trust issues—until h met Casey Thomas, the nanny he hired for his orphaned niece. Cas didn't trust men, period. But anything could happen in such close quarters—including an attraction neither could deny or resist!

#2002 ACCIDENTAL CINDERELLA—
Nancy Robards Thompson
Take the island paradise of St. Michel, stir in scandalously sexy celebrity chef Carlos Montigo and voilà, down-on-her-luck TV presenter Lindsay Preston had all the ingredients for a new lease on life. And boy, was Carlos ever a dish….

#2003 THE TEXAS CEO'S SECRET—Nicole Foster
The Foleys and the McCords
With his family's jewelry store empire on the skids, Blake McCord didn't have time to dabble in romance—especially with his brother' former fiancée, Katie Whitcomb-Salgar. Or was the heiress just wh the CEO needed to unlock his secret, sensual side?

#2004 DADDY ON DEMAND—Helen R. Myers
Left to raise twin nieces by himself, millionaire Collin Masters turned to his former—somewhat disgruntled—employee, Sabrina Sinclaire. She had no choice but to accept his job offer, and soon, his offer of love gave "help wanted" a whole new meaning….

SSECNMBPA090